Middle Murphy

ILLINOIS SHORT FICTION

A list of books in the series appears at the end of this volume.

Mark Costello

Middle Murphy

UNIVERSITY OF ILLINOIS PRESS

Urbana and Chicago

Publication of this work has been supported in part by a grant from the Illinois Arts Council, a state agency.

Illini Books edition, 1994
© 1991 by Mark Costello
Manufactured in the United States of America
1 2 3 4 5 C P 5 4 3 2 1

This book is printed on acid-free paper.

These stories appeared, sometimes in different forms and under different titles, in the following publications:

"Young Republican," *Missouri Review,* 3 (1982); *Black Warrior Review,* 9:1 (Fall 1982)
"The Soybean Capital of the World," *Story Quarterly,* 10–11 (1980)
"The Roaring Margaret," *Denver Quarterly,* 25:2 (Fall 1990)
"Forty-Hour Devotion," *TriQuarterly,* 71 (Winter 1988)
"Room 601," *Shenandoah,* 38:1 (1988)
"Finding My Niche," *Iowa Review,* 19:1 (1989)

Library of Congress Cataloging-in-Publication Data

Costello, Mark.
    Middle Murphy / Mark Costello.
        p.   cm.—(Illinois short fiction)
    ISBN 0-252-01795-1 (cloth: alk. paper); ISBN 0-252-06319-8 (paper: alk. paper)
    I. Title. II. Series.
    PS3553.O763M5   1991
    813'.54—dc20   90-27662
                                                                                      CIP

For my sister Mary Anne
and for my children, Jennifer, Katy,
Patrick, and Ivy Anna

Contents

Young Republican   1

The Soybean Capital of the World   29

The Roaring Margaret   75

Forty-Hour Devotion   87

Room 601   117

Finding My Niche   128

Young Republican

I SEE a truck and a paint brush. The paint brush belongs to Frankie Rumble. The truck, a flatbed with two flat tires and several rolls of black roofing paper stacked on the back and on the ground all around it, belongs to Frankie Rumble's unemployed and unemployable father.

Behind it, four years old and about to leave for Springfield, Illinois, and my first state fair, standing in a fragrance of axle grease and hollyhock shadow, dressed completely in white, white knee socks, white patent leather shoes, white sailor suit, I do my first friend my first favor. Because he is two years older and tells me I'd look better, because he has not only a brush but an opened bucket and wants to, I let Frankie Rumble paint me black.

It is a color that makes my mother cry. But not my father. Calmly, with a smile and even a laugh or two, he takes over the job of cleaning me up. As he scrubs me, as he ruffles my hair and asks me why I did it, why I let Frankie Rumble paint me black, I'm shamed both by his laughter and his kindness, I sense in the shadows of the house next door, all of the jobs and five-dollar bills with which my father has provided Frankie Rumble's perpetually broke and job-losing father, a generosity and patience I could this afternoon in the shadow of rolled roofing paper and a flatbed truck, only botch, not copy.

1

It's March, I guess. The wind is blowing and my father is precinct committeeman. Precinct headquarters is located in an unused room in the back of a barbershop. The barber pole turns red and white and a photograph of the Republican candidate for county coroner has been tacked to twenty-five or thirty white lath stakes arranged in a line on lawns in front of precinct headquarters. The face of the Republican candidate for county coroner is white. The face that appears now in the window of my father's car is black. Motioning through the glass, a young Negro asks my father if he can talk to him for a minute.

My father turns to me and says: "I'll be right back," then he's half a block away with his overcoat flapping in the wind. Now he and the young Negro are shaking hands and my father's nose is spurting blood. Backing away with his hands held up as if he is being robbed, my father turns toward me. His blood is bright and he is a long way from the car.

At night my father rubs my back. Above and all around the bed, there's a scent of liniment. Green, clean, dignified, confidential, it carries with it bouquets of booze, aromas of my father's old, mild drinking problem. As he rubs my back, my father says: *relax*, that word turning as always into *tall:* "If you're ever going to be *tall*," my father says, "you've got by golly to *stretch* yourself."

When he says this, I grab the headboard of my bed and my father grabs my ankles. Then he begins to pull. My wrists snap, my spine pops. Stretched out above the sheets, I cling to the headboard of my bed and my father hauls and staggers at my ankles.

When it falls, will the tree of paradise fall down upon my father? I think so, he doesn't. Squatting in its shadow, dressed in a Palm Beach suit and Panama hat, my father smokes a cigarette and talks politics with my sweating uncle. The sun is hot. The axe is blunt. The trunk is huge, malodorous. White ropes quiver and stiffen in the green leaves and now as the tree of paradise begins to squeak and tremble, I ask my father please to move. But he doesn't. Turning toward me, he smiles and tells me not to worry, to calm down, to go play ball. But I don't. I stand here on the sidewalk and I watch him.

A fact: my father was forty-eight years old when I was born. A result: he has always carried for me the fragility and gravity of the shined shoe, the snap-brim hat, the black droop of a silk sock against an ankle thin and dry as a white lath stake.

So it's March again, I guess. Election Day, Election Day. Even as twenty-five or thirty white lath stakes tremble in the wind in front of precinct headquarters, even as I rehearse and rehearse their trembling, a car door opens then slams shut and my father is sitting behind the wheel with a bloody handkerchief pressed to his face and I cannot take my eyes off his clothes. His hat is tipped back and I look at its silk band. From that I look to the silk of his tie and the silk lining of his overcoat and suit coat.

Sitting next to him, it's as if my own bones are being sewn with silk, a dignity and rage that will muffle and stuff each other, that will keep me too from ever throwing a punch, from ever hitting back.

When we get back to the house, my father refuses to remove his overcoat and hat. My mother keeps telling him to take off his overcoat and hat, but my father refuses. Standing at the window staring out into the street, his face beet red and his mustache silver, he looks like a man about to suffer a stroke. His hat seems less like a hat than a plug or stopper. About his necktie, suit and overcoat there is something roseate, woolen, silken and swollen, the equivalent in clothing of the hypertension from which he suffers.

As my father becomes more silent, grunting and humming through his broken nose, my mother begins to speak and explain. There's no one to blame, she says, except the Democrats. They are the ones who paid the Negro to punch him in the nose. "They just want to get," she tells my father again and again, "your name and picture in the papers."

As my father's silence deepens, as he seems to stare harder and harder out the window into the darkening day, his refusal to speak or to remove his overcoat and hat begins to frighten me. About his stance, there is a heedlessness and determination so small and stopped, it's as if his mood is about to occlude, as if it can result in nothing short of a stroke, one that my father will encourage and invite, one for which my mother will finally be to blame. When I think this thought, feel the misery and extremity of it, I see once more the Negro's grip of greeting, the arc of the fist as it whistles, blackens, intersects the nose, a handshake flung like blood from a cup into my father's face.

There are also the men who wait, behind the dark grillwork of banks all up and down our state to cash, if he wants them to, checks for my father: "Did you know," my father often tells me, "that there's not a town or city in this state where I couldn't, if I wanted to, cash a check?"

When my father says this, I breathe the aroma of his white port wine and see not only the bald and decent tellers, but the bankers, lawyers, engineers and industrialists who back them up, whole towns and darkening cities of tired and serious men who have come not only to trust but to depend upon my father, the map of our state shaped less by rivers or boundary lines than by the length, breadth and cartography of my father's credit, the men who will cash, if he wants them to, checks for my father.

The names are German names. Hans, Hiles, Fritz, Victor. From their names alone these kids seem to take the cue that makes them take things from me. First they take my pearl-handled pistols and lever-action Winchesters, later they take my footballs, basketballs, autographed baseballs. Though my father buys these things for me, it's my mother who keeps inventory. And she's the one who sends me out, "without fail young man," to bring them back.

Usually it's Saturday afternoon and I don't like this task. Nor do I like the smell of the house toward which I'm heading. Smelling at this hour of the mother's dumplings, it's a smell they've brought down somehow from Wisconsin.

Sniffing it, I follow it toward the closed back door. Before I'm halfway there, I hear what I knew I'd hear, the Saturday afternoon sound of someone blond being beaten in a basement. I can't help it, I'm thrilled and pulled into the shadows at the foundation of the house. Squatting, I hold my breath and listen to the razor strap. In its swish and whomp there is a suggestion of the forge and foundry. I know if I looked through the window, I'd see an unconverted coal furnace down there with a grate of blue teeth glowing in the dark.

Before I can look, though, the back door slams open half a foot from my face. I rise in a cloud of sauerkraut. It's as if the mother's hair is made of sauerkraut. She's wearing a hairnet and there are large dark stars of sauerkraut sweat below both her arms. She has b.o. and she has it plenty. She weighs maybe two hundred or two hundred and twenty-five pounds and the heels of her shoes look like the heads of battered hammers.

Before and below her, in undershirt and five o'clock shadow, stands the bald father. His jaw is blue, his chest is thin and hairy. His ears are hairy. In his pale breastbone there is something pinched and vicious to which no one, not even the mother, can appeal. At night I've heard her shriek, the whole house shake with the father's tiny fury, authority.

He steps toward me. He is shorter than I am and from his right hand dangles the razor strap. In his left hand, delicately and uncertainly, as if it is not in his nationality to touch it, he holds my football with the white night stripes still clean and new near both its noses.

Raising it, he points it at my throat and says: "Does this belong to you?"

When I shake my head and say, "No it doesn't," a face appears on the basement stairs. The face belongs to Hans, Hiles, Fritz or Victor, and I can't look away from it until Mr. Schultz or Mr. Schmidt steps a little closer and says: "Then why did Mrs. Murphy call here and say that it belonged to you?"

Though I know my name is Murphy, though I know the man is talking about my mother, I can't immediately tell the lie I know I'm going to tell. I'm still looking at Hans, Hiles, Fritz or Victor and do not answer until Mr. Schultz or Mr. Schmidt whispers: "Answer me."

Answering him, I lower my eyes and call into question my mother's mentality, tell him she must have called the wrong number, must have gotten the wrong name. Elliptic, lame, my lie seems to hang in the air in front of me. Cutting through it, Mr. Schultz or Mr. Schmidt makes his move. With a swiftness like a fist hitting my ribs, he slams the football into my chest.

"Here," he says, "you take this and get out of here."

I am about to protest, about to offer it back, when Mrs. Schultz or Mrs. Schmidt stomps a foot and hisses: "Scat."

Like a halfback hitting a line, I take off across their lawn. But if my kitchen and my mother become, as I run, a kind of goal line or awful end zone, I do not score, do not deliver. Because I cannot pass, when I get there, my dark garage.

In it, I find all the tools I need. With a steel brush, sandpaper and a can of turpentine, I scratch, sand and stain it until no one, not even my mother, could any longer call my football mine. Against a temptation to hide up there myself, I unfold the step-ladder and climb to the rafters, tuck my football away in a snarl of torn hornet, wasp and bird nests, a dust of rusted screens and shattered storm doors.

Slamming open the back door, pounding up the stairs, I try to get through the kitchen without talking to my mother. But when I enter it, she's doing something that scares and stops me. On the stove she's cooking soap; slivers and chips of white Ivory, green Palmolive, red Life Buoy and brown Fels-Naptha no longer large enough to use. The fire is blue, the pot is wobbling. From it comes a smell of thrift and fish. Though I know once it's hot enough, she'll pour the pot boiling into the toilet, it's as if this time my mother's going to wash out my mouth instead, scrub out the lies I'm set to tell about my missing football.

But she won't let me say a word. Staring at my empty hands, she shakes her head, tightens her eyes. When I begin to speak, to tell her that the football at the Schultzes' or the Schmidts' wasn't even mine, she steps across the kitchen and says: "Shush. Don't say a word. You get, young man, right into your room."

My mother, though, can't keep from following me into my room. Just as I sit down on the bed, the door flies open and she rushes through with her pot of smoking soap. It's a strange sight, full of fog and nausea. For a moment, it's as if she's carrying something that I've done, a pot that I've been sick in. In the bath-room, when she flips it upside down, I feel for a second that it's me in there, coughing, heaving, fouling the bowl. Without rais-ing or turning her head, as if she's talking to someone in the toilet, she whispers: "You get in here this very minute, young man, I want to talk to you."

When I enter the bathroom, my mother rises from her scrub-bing. With the long-handled toilet brush still dripping from her hand, she says: "Do you know, young man, how many footballs *in the last year and a half alone* your father's bought for you?"

I know the answer. The answer's three. But because my

7

mother seems to want to tell me herself, I let her: "I'll tell you the answer," she says, "the answer is *three*. If you don't believe me, I'll show you the bills and the canceled checks."

Like bills or canceled checks, like minnows or slips of glycerin fish, like pale price tags for all the footballs that my father has bought and I have lost, my mother's soap floats in the toilet.

But she won't let me look at it for long. "Don't you think," she whispers and twists my chin toward her, "that this football business has gone far enough?"

Though I do not say a word, my agreement is so complete, my mother releases me, sends me with a shove back into my room. Stretched out across my bed, I feel sick and dizzy in a way that seems to include my father. Like a sieve or heaving horn of plenty, I feel his generosity pass through me. Not just footballs, but the whole string of bats, basketballs, cap pistols, slingshots and sailboats by which I have, for years, been buying and surviving my neighborhood, the blond kids, the thin fathers and the basement beatings, a patronage and politics in which my father, Republican County Chairman, steadily and quietly, backs and supports me.

But my mother doesn't. Bursting into my room, she issues her ultimatum: "All right, young man," she whispers, "if you won't go over there and get that football, I, Lord help me, will."

But I know she won't. Because if she did, she might somehow draw my father into it. And if he ever went over to the Schultzes' or the Schmidts', he'd never come back. His clothes alone would kill him. Against the suets and sauerkrauts of their kitchen, his hat, suit and tie would hiss, shrivel, shrink. Falling onto bald linoleum in front of their kitchen sink, he'd fall at the same time into bad publicity. Tomorrow morning not only his name, but his picture would appear on the front page of the paper.

Since she doesn't move from the spot where she stands, my mother seems to sense this too. Filling with tears, her eyes look blue, youthful. Pinned to the bed by the lies she would not let me tell about it, I imagine her striding back from the Schultzes' or the Schmidts' with my football tucked in the crook of her arm. When my mother feels me feeling this, imagining myself somehow older than she is, she says: "All right, young man, just wait until your father gets home."

When my father gets home, though, my mother doesn't say a word to him. Throughout supper we observe a silence that won't complete itself, I know, until recovering my football from the garage, engaging in a game of catch designed before long to exclude me, I can walk away from Hans, Hiles, Fritz and Victor, can turn at the head of the driveway and watch a football that my father bought for me, being tossed back and forth, back and forth, at the far end of the block.

Clotheshorse is a term with which I've had for a long time, a lot of trouble. Used first by a nun in a cloakroom scolding, used too often and freely by aunts and uncles to describe what I'm turning myself into, used again and again by my mother to bemoan the bills I've been running up, *clotheshorse* is something I spend a lot of time telling myself I'm not.

But I am. I'm a clotheshorse. And if my mother has, as she always says she does, the bills and the canceled checks to prove it, I have the tissue paper.

This tissue paper comes in shiny black and gold boxes from men's stores called Bachrach's and Plum's and Loeb's and because it serves as wadding and padding for shirts and sweaters and slacks that aren't the least bit breakable, this tissue paper makes me nervous. Looking at it, at how white and tufted and vaguely edible it looks, I think that if they graze on anything, clotheshorses graze on tissue paper.

Sometimes sitting alone in a bedroom strewn with tissue paper, I imagine a whole herd of clotheshorses grazing on tissue paper strewn along the curbs in front of Bachrach's, Plum's and

Loeb's and, my eyes glazing over, I can't keep my hands off the tissue paper. Balling it up, hand packing it as tightly as I can, I imagine hurling it, with a rock wrapped inside, at the full-length, three-way mirror in front of which this afternoon I've stood admiring myself in my new purchases from Bachrach's, Plum's and Loeb's, sending with a smashing of glass, a whole herd of clotheshorses clattering along the streets of downtown Decatur.

I am twelve years old and starting to get hit a lot in the stomach. Not just tapped, but slugged. The afternoon, for instance, that Thomas E. Dewey comes to town. On a crowded railroad siding, one foot on the rail and one foot off, wearing the white helmet liner and black-lettered T-shirt of the Decatur Junior Police, a smell of steam and cinders in the air, anxious for Thomas E. Dewey's train to arrive, telling myself that Thomas E. Dewey is on a whistle-stop tour, liking the idea of Thomas E. Dewey being on a whistle-stop tour, I'm talking to another Junior Policeman, a fellow member of the honor guard, a red-headed kid with freckles on his face, freckles on his fists.

His name is either Schultz or Schmidt and when he hits me, it's the middle of summer, sometime around sunset on Saturday night, the hot fans of a hatchery sending a smell of feathers and incubators into the street. On his right fist, in ballpoint, the kid has drawn a swastika with black strikes of lightning just above and just below it.

His name is either Hiles or Fritz and when he throws his fist, I'm in an alley or beside the bleachers at Fan's Field or in a lunch line or under, say, the well-lit entrance of the Friday Night Dance at the YMCA. Broad-shouldered, either blond or red-headed, he's often freckled, always German and when he hits me in the stomach, my breath seems to blow the hat right off my father's head.

Young Republican

Shocked, sucking for breath, I stagger backward and can still see the curb. The way my father staggers along the curb toward me. Then the door opens and slams shut and my father's sitting behind the wheel of the car with a bloody handkerchief pressed to his face and I myself have stumbled home.

After quiet, in search of a silence in which to refuse an excuse I've already accepted too often and too easily, I lie atop my bed. Though I know the hat and the handkerchief are a lie, that my father's got nothing to do with the gyms and incinerators where I get hit again and again in the stomach, I feel at the same time an overcoat tightening around my shoulders, feel less each time like I've been hit than haunted: when the fist touches my stomach, the hat jumps off my father's head. Staggering backward, sucking for breath, I can neither excuse nor blame my father. I can do nothing, it seems, but resemble him.

It's a resemblance that lights late tonight, the light above the bathroom mirror. Using a mirror from one of my mother's dusty compacts, I study my profile until I find within it, not so much the dignity and sincerity of my father, as the bones and lips of someone even I would like to hit, not only in the stomach, but in the mouth, nose, over the head right now with a whistling wrench as well.

I am a junior and so is it. My father's favorite liniment. *Absorbine Jr.* Green-black, with an antique, green-black, fin de siècle scent, every bottle bears an illustration. The illustration is an illustration of an infected foot. The wound is located between the big and second toe. Ovoid, biblical, bubonic, red, it's the kind of wound my sister's going to get when, staying out too late some night, she'll be walking down the street and somebody will sneak up behind her and hit her over the head.

I have, it's true, a sister. But she doesn't live with us. She lives alone behind her bedroom door, eating peanut butter sandwiches, drinking Coke, listening to her radio. She is a senior in high school and if she doesn't watch out, she's going to fool around and get hit some night over the head.

Though it's my father's sentiment, he seems to convey it less with words than grunts and wafts of green-black liniment. In the white square of his white bedroom door, his toes white and root-like, his trousers rolled to show his white and ivory ankles, he bends above a white bath mat, anoints his chalk white feet with sweet *Absorbine Jr.* Hovering before him, my mother shakes a finger at my sister.

Caught at the front door midway through another of the swift, silent exits she tries to make most every evening, my sister stands flushed and defiant. For five nights running, she's tried to leave the house with too much lipstick on, with a sweater too tight or a skirt too short, last night without a slip, tonight without saying what time they can expect her home.

But my father won't hear of it. Shaking his head and bending over even lower, he blows on his toes and my mother seems to lift toward my sister whispering: "Do you know, young lady, what your father said? He said: 'She's going to fool around some night and get hit over the head.'"

"Get hit over the head," my sister hisses, "what does he mean I'll *get hit over the head?*"

What my father means, I do not know, cannot exactly say. But not long after my sister slams the door upon a promise to be home at least by eleven, I close my door, go to bed and dream a dream in which it's a little after eleven and a wind of liniment blows against my sister.

But she doesn't care. Even as I whisper, "Hurry, Martha, please hurry," her broken promise breaks in blood and burlap above her head. Because she's asked for it, my sister incurs a wound like the wound on a bottle of *Absorbine Jr.*

Slamming door after door, my pale father staggers at eleven forty-five (by the luminescent bedside clock) through my room into the bathroom, his undershorts baggy, his knees bony, his ankles tiny, a scent of liniment so strong I follow him in to pee. Peeing to the hum of her radio, the top of a Coke bottle popping, I tell myself that, though forty-five minutes late, my sister is safe. But it does no good. Falling asleep for a second time, I watch once more her scalp divide, see her again and again as some Cinderella of the monkey wrench and gunnysack, cannot all night long stop whispering: "Hurry, Martha, please *hurry.*"

Under palm fronds that arc over the spare tire, under holy water kits and Scotch plaid bags full of old road flares and bent St. Christopher medals, under the jack, under stack after stack of *American Legion* magazines, I find them. And when I do so, I not only open and touch them, week after week, I borrow them.

Afterward, I wash my hands and imagine the man. The one who frames my father. The sly clerk in a low hotel, the acne-scarred agent of the Democratic party who plants each week dirty magazines in the trunk of my father's car.

Now as the twelve bells of noon release the faithful, I feel my mother and father starting home from church. Less, sweet Jesus, than a block and a half away. Slamming the back of my fist against my forehead, I try to remember the order in which to restack the magazines before I return them. But I can't. Rattled, I stack a *Flash* atop a *Nude* atop a *Pin-up* atop a *Vue.* Snapping the stolen car keys from the back of the basement toilet, I unlock the door and rush toward the garage. Adrift in a dream of acne and moonlight, the deft Democrat who plants not only dirty magazines but, I pray, TNT in the trunk of the car, I make the same wish I wish each time I stash the magazines: that this time as my mother and father round the corner, as I slam the trunk lid down like a plunger, the roof will lift off the garage. In a ton of TNT both I and all the magazines, each squeaking garter and nyloned thigh, each glittering lip and lolling tongue will go up in groans and smoke, final white atonement for this treachery I commit most every Sunday morning against my smiling, waving and returning father.

Then one Sunday morning, something odd begins to happen. The dirty magazines begin to disappear. Their disappearance is slow, decent, diplomatic. One week a *Vue* or two is gone, the next a *Nude*, the third a *Pin-up*, until at last only a *Flash* is left, then it too is gone. The Sunday morning when I search the trunk of the car and find it completely empty of dirty magazines, my father takes me for a drive that seems to last all afternoon long. When we are a little way out of town, my father explains to me what he has explained to me before: what he does to stay awake while driving alone.

Asking me to pretend that I'm not here, that he's driving alone and the roads are slick with rain or ice and it's almost dark, my father performs a kind of pantomime. Nodding like somebody about to fall asleep at the wheel, he talks about the telephone poles along the side of the highway, about how, when he starts getting sleepy, he uses the telephone poles like rosary beads.

It's an old habit of his, peaceful, reflective, private. The handkerchief in his lapel pocket is scented with Mennen's, his hands are on the wheel, his shirt is white, his tie shot with blue, the dashboard with its ever-silent radio seems somehow tabernacular. Pocked black with birds, the telephone lines loop outward. Each telephone pole we pass, my father ticks off a prayer, a "Glory be" or "Jesus, Mary, Joseph, pray for us," each prayer he prays ripping off a page from a dirty magazine, the tappets and crankshaft shredding and screwing it through the engine, shooting it charred, ruffled and black from the exhaust, the ash of some awful lesson lifting and fluttering in the wind behind my father, the highway he drives a path I know I'm going to find, from this day forward, more and more difficult to follow.

This is high school. This is football practice. I am a thirteen-year-old freshman and my father is driving me toward our first contact session. We are going this morning, as our coach puts it, to "put on the war bonnets" and my father has a few words to say about it. He doesn't much like football, he tells me, because football doesn't much like our family. Documenting this, he tells me not only about Uncle Tim's triple hernia and Uncle Jim's ruptured spleen, about Cousin Jack's detached retina and Nephew Matt's shattered mastoid, but about something darker, too.

Deep, chronic, inoperable, a matter of floating kidneys, ringing ears and double vision, football injuries have a way in our family of bringing on alcoholism. As we pull into the high school parking lot, my father speaks not only the names of my uncles and cousins who have become alcoholics as the result of football injuries, but the names of the state institutions in which these uncles and cousins have died or are still living, if, he tells me, you could call it living.

But I open the door of the car anyway and my father stops me long enough to shake my hand and say: "Take it easy son. And whatever you do, don't go out there and get yourself hurt."

Walking toward the locker room, I feel as if through my conversation with my father, I've already gone out there and gotten myself hurt. Inside, I feel rigged with crystal fractures just waiting to shatter and happen, the whole history of our family's football fragility embodied in my knee-knocking body.

But I walk into the locker room anyway and under the orange helmet, clammy pads and chafing straps of the Screaming Eagles of St. Cecelia's, I listen to our coach scream about the Big Head. Sure, this is a winning football team with twenty-two returning starters, sure this is a winning football *program* we've all worked hard to put together, but if we get the Big Head, our coach tells us, we can forget about it.

Trying to forget about what my father has just told me concerning football and our family, I look at our coach. Heavy and swarthy, a man of butt-sprung trousers, white saliva, blackboards and bits of broken chalk, our coach is an Italian with very broad shoulders and a very small head.

I, on the other hand, am an Irishman with very narrow shoulders and a very large head. I am telling myself that without any help from the outside, I've already *got* the Big Head, when, having received the signal to take to the field, my teammates with their clacking cleats leave five-pronged black tar tracks on the concrete floor.

For three long weeks I smell the smell these tracks give off. In it, there is a hint of brimstone, benzoin, alcohol and danger. Breathing it, I seem to catch a whiff of my own insides, something that keeps me at the back of the line.

This is tackling practice and I am looking for a friend. Across from me, also hanging back, I find him in Ambrose Horan. Large-headed, narrow-shouldered, Irish and anxious to please, Ambrose understands as I understand, how to rig and fix a collision so that it looks, but is not real. When he carries the ball, I tackle him; when I carry the ball, he tackles me. For three long weeks we accommodate and despise each other, until at last one afternoon we collide so softly our coach asks us to get up and try it again. When he claps his hands, we converge so slowly, he doesn't stop asking us to get up and try it again until, to the clapping of his hands Ambrose Horan is crying and I find my shoulder pads in my hands.

In their weight and shape there is something winged, familial. As he accepts them on this the morning after the night of my bilateral decision with my father to quit the football team, my coach, marking me as *nothing but a goddamned politician,* speaks finally the words he's been thinking, he tells me, for three weeks now: *You want so bad to be one of the guys don't you? Well if you want to know what I think, Murphy,* he says, *I think you're not only a quitter and full of bull, I think you're just plain yellow.*

She is black and he is fat. A fisherman, he tells me. Buffalo, carp, channel cat. For five dollars and a six-pack of Canadian Ace Extra Strong beer, he closes the bedroom door on us. On her dressing table there are several large, unmarked bottles of what look to be green perfume. On the wall, a picture of a bird with musical notes rising yellow from its yellow bill.

Hours afterward, behind the locked door of our basement bathroom, I drip iodine on the head of my penis, do a little dance, vomit and write the next day, a poem that ends with the following lines:

> So I left her up there
> in her green-smelling nest,
> Hail the conquering harlot,
> Consumattum est.

Though I do not show this poem to my father, though I burn it as soon as I've written it, it's as if somehow my father has read it. Because that very day, sitting on the front porch, noting the dark circles under my eyes, my father says: "Be careful, son, of the company you keep. You can always tell a man," he says, "by the company he keeps."

This is college. This is August. I am a seventeen-year-old freshman and my father is driving me this morning to the first session of Orientation Week. He is dressed in a Palm Beach suit and Panama hat and when I tell him I'm thinking about joining a fraternity, his mood turns shy, advisory.

Touching his thumb and index finger to the brim of his hat, he shakes his head. Looking straight up the highway, he tells me what he's read about fraternity deaths and cripplings from falls off cliffs and railroad trestles, one fraternity boy blinded and another fraternity boy electrocuted. Then my father speaks words that I will not forget: "Fool around with that fraternity stuff son," he says, "and you might wind up with your name and picture in the papers."

Even as he speaks his warning, a wooden paddle seems to crack across my ass and there is a blindfold tied tight around my head. I have lipstick on and I am wearing a Kotex. I am dressed in a gunnysack and there is a blind robin hanging from a string around my neck. This is Hell Night of Hell Week, about seven months later, and I have been herded along with the rest of my pledge brothers into the basement of our fraternity house.

When the actives slip the blindfold from my eyes, I can see nothing at first but the blue teeth of a furnace. Then someone points a shadeless floor lamp at my face and says: "Do you see this lamp and light bulb Murphy?"

"Yes."

"Can you see that it's plugged in?"

"Yes."

Then they turn it on and off and ask if I saw that too.

"Yes."

Can I see, someone asks me, the water running under the bedsprings?

"Yes."

"Lay down on the bedsprings Murphy."

I do what I am told.

"Can you hear the water running Murphy?"

"Yes."

"Do you know what water does to electricity Murphy," someone says, "it *conducts* the fucking stuff."

Then from behind me a hand unscrews the lighted lightbulb and they thrust the empty socket in front of my face. At the moment that the blindfold tightens once more across my eyes, someone says: "All right Murphy stick your finger in the socket."

As I raise my hand from the bedsprings, I know the upper-classmen intend only to initiate not to electrocute me. But I cannot help myself. As I move my index finger forward, I imagine my Kotex flaming, lipstick crackling, a dead and smelly little fish hopping up and down on my chest. On the front page of my hometown paper, in the headline and the picture, in the naming of my name and my father's name, in the words: *fraternity, mishap, prank* and *tragedy,* in the line *Michael Murphy, Jr., son of Area Supervisor for the State Employment Service and current Republican county chairman Michael "Mike" Murphy,* my father's warning will find its confirmation.

But when I finally stick my finger into it, the empty socket does not illuminate, it merely defines me: an eighteen-year-old freshman pledge, very very anxious to go along with the game, to get Hell Week over, to become at the end of the semester, if my grades hold up, oh happy thought, *one of the brothers.*

Her name is Laura, but she neither looks nor cooks like any Laura. A queen of grease, a Circe of cartilage and cabbage, she seems to specialize in pork. Night after night, noon after noon, she feeds us pork in barbecues, beans, casseroles, fat red dripping ribs. Though much of it is Negro food, Laura, who is not Negro, who is large and pale and comes from Wisconsin, makes it taste somehow Germanic. Broad in the shoulders, wide in the snout, my fraternity brothers (for I am now an active) huff, snuff, suck down Laura's food. And sometimes after supper of, say, a Friday or Saturday night, gathering around her drinking beer, throwing their arms around Laura's thick, wet neck, breathing in the atmosphere of her tattoos and armpits, they sing:

> My gal's a corker,
> She's a New Yorker,

I buy her everything to
keep her in style.
She's got a
paira legs,
Just like two whiskey kegs,
Yeh, boys, that's where my
money goes.

It goes without saying, I guess, that Laura and I don't get along. I mistrust her mustache, hairnets and hairy legs. Though a *her* instead of a *him*, there is something of the bugler and the barracks, of the squawk box and squad bay in Laura, a fondness for dinner gongs so loud and breakfast whistles so shrill and piping (I'm now in Naval ROTC), I sometimes think of Laura as a chief petty officer of pork, a tech sergeant of trichinosis.

The fraternity house itself contributes to this. Vast, Victorian and poor in its plumbing, it holds but three working stools, all in the fourth-floor toilet. When she's drunk enough beer to feel the need to go, Laura has to climb four floors to do so.

Forming a processional, the brothers float Laura out of the kitchen, across the dining room, through the library, up the stairs. Her weight shakes the chandeliers. At the second-floor landing, crossing into cloister, she begins to bray and obey an unwritten law I know she loves.

Each floor she attains, she speaks out her sex. "Woman on second!" she screams. "Woman on third! Woman on fourth!" Against the high-ceilinged halls, Laura's assertion of her sex seems high-pitched, hectic, hysterical. The more she bellows and howls that she's a woman on second, third or fourth, the more I tend to doubt that she's a woman at all. Such doubts do not amuse me, though, they frighten me. Sometimes when Laura screams, "Woman on second," the words "corker" and "New Yorker" spring into my mind. Though I know Laura doesn't hail from County Cork, that she's probably never even been to New

York, the words nonetheless horrify me. Above a pair of legs just like two whiskey kegs, I see a sex of staves, spigots and steam leaks. If she ever caught you in the center stall of the fourth-floor toilet, writing with black Magic Marker

> For a real drink
> To mess you up
> Mix Laura's pee
> With Sani-Flush

she'd make you pay the price for it.

I'm trying tonight to consider the paying of that price, when I hear Laura scream: "Woman on third!" Pocketing my black Magic Marker, I slam out of the center stall of the fourth-floor toilet, just as Laura screams: "Woman on fourth!"

When I hit the hall, most of the brothers have leather-thonged wooden paddles gripped in their fists. Bowing at the waist, dipping their paddles like swords, they usher Laura into the fourth-floor toilet. With a curtsy and a flicker of thick ankle, she disappears into the center stall.

It is a disappearance that draws our ears to the door. With my ear jammed against the door, with a grin on my face and my nostrils pinched between my thumb and index finger, I bend forward and try so hard not to laugh or make a sound, my effort somehow sounds and questions what I'm doing: sometimes swaying in the kitchen with an arm around Laura's neck, or pressed with my brothers against the door of the fourth-floor toilet, I think of my father and what he'd think of me now, this company of brothers I seem to have to work so hard to keep.

With a Lucky Strike stuck in the corner of her mouth, Laura keeps sticking her head out of the kitchen door, keeps pointing at the mistletoe above her head, keeps asking who's going to give her a great big Christmas kiss. Sitting at a corner table of the dining room, my plate filled with untouched fat and pork and sauerkraut, I can't take my eyes off Laura.

When I rise from the table, I neither know why I do it, nor why it seems my responsibility to do it. But the brothers seem to sense my inclination too. Looking up from their plates of fat and pork and sauerkraut, they regard me with their blue and tiny eyes. Then the tables are empty and all of the brothers are behind me and all around me and there is a grin on my face and sweat on my brow. In the kitchen door, Laura stands with one hand on her hip. When I kiss her, she throws her arms around my neck. And it's not until I've tapped her teeth with my teeth that Laura releases me, offers to my ear, her throaty malediction: "Merry Christmas Murphy," she whispers, "you sweet old Anta Santa you."

The Anta Santa is not a wind. Nor is it any anti-Christ. The Anta Santa is, instead, a sophomore, and, among the members of my fraternity, an old, if somewhat oddly named tradition. I don't know who came up with the term Anta Santa or why. But I do know this. Each year just before Finals Week, which comes just before Christmas Vacation, we have a Christmas party. Although it concludes with a stag movie thrown onto a yellow bed sheet above the crescents, columns and pseudo-Egyptian claptrap of the chapter room, the main event comes earlier in the evening with the annual naming of the Anta Santa. From among the members of the sophomore class, the class traditionally toughest on them, the freshman pledges choose and name as Anta Santa the man they most, each year, despise.

I am this year a sophomore and so afraid of being chosen Anta Santa, I'm sitting in the living room with my back against the fireplace. Each brick behind me bears the chiseled nickname of one of my brothers. My brothers have named each other names like Howdy, Toady, Humper, Hairs, Tank and Truck.

Now a brass dinner gong is struck, a bank of kleig lights

flashes on and the freshman pledges burst through the double doors at the front of the crowded living room. This is the beginning of the Christmas party, this is a "line-up," the lights along these walls are from the army or the police department.

One by one my classmates are called forward. With paddles in their fists, with the thongs of paddles wrapped around their wrists, the freshman pledges call forth fellow sophomores Howdy, Toady, Humper, Hairs, Tank, then finally Truck. Chucking him under the chin, the pledges call Truck a *prickshitsadistbarbariananimalasshole,* until it seems at last that he's their man, that my wait is almost over, that they are about to name brother Truck this year's Anta Santa.

With my back pressed against the fireplace, I try my best to do so, but cannot quite control my relief. *Let it be him,* I think again and again, *let it be him.* But even as I think the thought, the entire freshman pledge class turns toward me. Caught with a grin on my face, all I can see is teeth. "Murphy," they scream, "get your ass up here."

Though I try to hurry, it takes me a long time to get my ass up there. On my way up there, weaving through my assembled brothers, I try to get the grin off my face, but the grin on my face seems to slow, fix, convict me. These last four months I've been up to my old tricks, playing politics, loaning out to the freshman pledges, sweaters, shirts, cuff links, cummerbunds and five-dollar bills, running a kind of campaign in reverse, trying so hard in every way I can think of *not* to be named this year's Anta Santa, trying so hard now to get my ass up there, to get this over with, I stumble over one of my brothers and feel not only the black slap of a paint brush across my gut, but a clapping of hands that sends me once more into the arms of Ambrose Horan, feel a pair of football shoulder pads in my hands, hear words that make my going even slower: *You want so bad to be one of the guys don't you? Well if you want to know what I think, Murphy, I think you're not only a quitter and full of bull, I think you're just plain yellow.*

Which is the color, appropriately, of the sweater he's got on.

The spokesman, that is, who the freshman pledges have elected tonight to speak to me. Though I'm braced at attention, staring according to custom straight into the bank of klieg lights in front of me, I can see that he is blond and freckled, wide not only in the cheekbones, but in the nostrils too.

When he clears his throat, he speaks not only for himself, he tells me, but for every single member of the freshman pledge class: *All twenty-goddamned-six of them.*

Taking a step toward me, he places a hand above his heart and wants to know if I recognize the sweater he's got on. Though the sweater he's got on is a V-necked Bernard Altman that I bought at Bachrach's, Plum's, or Loeb's, I neither nod nor shake my head.

So he says: "Very well then we'll refresh your memory for you, Murphy." Raising his paddle, he whispers: "One, two, three," and the entire freshman pledge class screams: "That god-damned sweater belongs to you."

As do, it seems, a number of the clothes they're wearing. This goes slow, this is a kind of a strip show. One by one the pledges step forward to pull off and drop at my feet, clothes I've loaned them and not bothered to get back. The last item that they drop, though, is not a piece of clothing, it's a black Magic Marker.

It looks a lot like the one with which, in the center stall of the fourth-floor toilet, I wrote:

> For a real drink
> To mess you up,
> Mix Laura's pee
> With Sani-Flush

In his right hand, the spokesman for the freshman pledge class holds a beer mug. It is filled, he tells me, with piss and Sani-Flush.

His proposal is a modest one. All I have to do *not* to be named this year's Anta Santa, is to chug (he proffers it to me) this little elixir.

About his offer there is something of the bedspring and the empty light socket, the notoriety and finality one might find by sticking a finger into it. If there really *is* Sani-Flush in the ammoniac and bubbly mug he holds up to me, my downing of it might just make the front page of my hometown newspaper.

Not even I, however, want that badly *not* to be named this year's Anta Santa. So I shake my head, the French doors are thrown open, an elixir of piss and putative Sani-Flush, my only way out, flies out steaming into the falling snow.

This snow is lovely, this snow is thick, this snow is falling on Highway 66. Highway 66 leads to California and the anonymity I right now long for. But I do not watch this snow fall on Highway 66. I watch it swirl and fall instead on Highway 10, a highway that, taking me forty-five miles home to my parents' house in Decatur, seems to lead me across our snow-deep lawn, to lift my hand toward my mother's frozen bedroom window.

Pressing hard against its frame, trying to muffle a vibration I fear might wake my father, I tap lightly three times on the glass.

When she unlocks and opens the front door, my mother says: "Whatever you do, Michael, don't wake your father."

Setting my duffel bag down, I follow her to the lighted nightstand.

"My God Michael," she says, "it's two o'clock in the morning. Why aren't you at school? What are you doing home at this hour?"

Strained, pale, her face tempts me to tell her that I've been named this year's Anta Santa and that I'm quitting school, but I do not do so.

Instead, I tell her that I missed the last bus, so I hitchhiked home.

"Do you mean, Michael," she says, "that you hitchhiked forty-five miles in the middle of the night?"

It is a question that awakens my father. But my mother doesn't let him up. She doesn't even let him get out of bed. Leaning into his room and blocking his door, she says: "Yes Mike, it's Michael. He hitchhiked home. Now you pull up those covers. You go right back to sleep."

An hour later, with both of them asleep, I lie in bed and think about my father. Twice he has staggered ghostlike and storklike through my room to the toilet. Twice I have resisted the temptation to follow him in to pee. But like underwear hung white-on-white on a low clothesline across my room, I cannot erase his double passage.

Silent, indelible, it tells me what my father wouldn't want to know, what my father wouldn't want to hear about. And he would not, I know, want to hear about tonight, a ritual of klieg lights, piss and Sani-Flush for which I feel right now unable to account, except to say, I seem to have been named this year's Anta Santa without ever having left this house.

In my father's house, there are many mansions, institutions. This armory is one of them.

My shoes this morning are white. So are my socks, underwear, blouse and cover. "Blouse" and "cover" are military terms for jacket and hat. But they also catch and cover pretty exactly an old-sailor-suit sense of how this morning I am dressed.

Standing behind a parade stand in a high-domed, sky-lighted armory, I'm about to leave this morning not for Springfield, Illinois, and my first state fair, but for Quantico, Virginia, and the U.S. Marine Corps.

Having stuck for three years with Naval ROTC, having spent the summer between my junior and senior years in Platoon Leader's Class, having received this morning not only my bachelor's degree, but my commission, I'm now Second Lieutenant Michael Murphy, Jr., USMCR, 075519. Also, I'm about to receive my first salute.

When a freshly commissioned second lieutenant receives from an enlisted man his first salute, it is customary that he return that salute with the handing over of a dollar bill. This is the very stuff of which my father's sense of fair America is made. And besides, over the years, quietly backing and supporting the politics I've played, my father has handed me over a number of dollar bills. For that matter, a number also of five, ten, and twenty dollar bills. So it is only right that the pockets of my dress whites be deep and immaculate, but empty.

They are. When I explain to him what the portly chief petty officer standing just outside the big, double, truckwide doors of the armory expects of me, my father is only too happy to oblige. Handing over a very crisp one dollar bill, he steps back to watch. So, holding tightly to her purse, does my mother. So, somewhere I guess, does the spirit of Frankie Rumble.

The salute itself should be a simple matter, but for me, it isn't. First comes the salute, then the returning of it, then the handing over of the dollar bill. I, however, slur the sequence a bit. Under the pressure of my father's pleasure, the size and whiteness of a cover that makes my head feel even bigger than it is, my shoulders even narrower than they are, I'm a little quick with the buck. Partly this has to do with the man himself. With his gut and his mustache, with his tiny and hungover-looking eyes, the chief looks not only petty and porcine, he looks, as he flips his cigarette away, a little like Laura letting go of a Lucky. Also, like Laura, he's quick on the uptake. Taking me up on my mistake, he palms my father's dollar bill and then not only salutes, but rebukes me: "You don't have to pay me to salute you sir," he says, "it's my *duty* to salute you sir."

Though he speaks them loud enough for my parents to hear, the chief's words do not double my father over with laughter.

Nor do they make my mother cry. Instead, walking arm-in-arm into a late May morning, my parents come out of the armory to congratulate me. Behind their backs, however, the chief is pocketing my father's dollar bill and somewhere in the bushes at the base of the armory I feel Frankie Rumble crouching, bucket and brush in hand, ready to paint, if I'd let him, not only me and my dress whites, but every salute I'll ever receive, a glittering, obliterating black.

The Soybean Capital of the World

MAYBE it was a Dodge, black and battered, or maybe it was a Buick, bulbous and blue. Maybe it was a memory or maybe it was a myth, one upon which Murphy had always to insist, one his mother had always to resist. "Come on Mom," he'd tell her, "you remember don't you? Dad and I were sitting in the car in front of precinct headquarters and . . . ," while his mother shook her head and said she didn't want to talk about it, Murphy could still see his father sitting behind the wheel with a bloody handkerchief pressed to his face.

Then they were home and his father was standing at the window, refusing to remove his overcoat and hat. When Murphy looked away from him, he felt his father's rage inflate too late along the silk linings of his overcoat and hat, wished that his father's fist would crash the glass, the two of them move out to search the streets not for his assassin, but the stealthy Democrats who, seeking bad publicity, his father's name and picture in the papers, paid the Negro to punch his father in the nose.

But after awhile, after his father had stood too long at the living room window, Murphy knew that his mother was right. They must calm down, no good could come from violence, *they just want our names and pictures in the papers,* there was nothing to be done. There in the middle of their darkened living room they were throttled and stopped. The only thing that could move or stir was his father's blood pressure. And the only way that that could go was up.

It must have been, Murphy often thought, upward of twenty-five years ago that that happened. And he was beginning to be ashamed of the way he asked his mother about it. Or more precisely, ashamed of how much he enjoyed asking his mother about it. For the most part he'd ask her about it only when he'd been drinking. But he drank heavily when he visited his parents' house, so much sometimes that he hardly ate any dinner at all. Often he would still be drinking when his mother had cleared the table and was washing the dishes and that was when he'd ask her about it, when he'd try to get her to talk about how, some twenty-five years ago on a wet and windy March election day, a squat and powerfully built young Negro had punched his father, then precinct committeeman, square in the nose. When he'd drunk enough, Murphy's curiosity would often narrow and focus solely on the make of the car. That was the single detail that he could not get straight, that eluded all elaboration, embroidery and rehearsal, a detail that made him look up from his third or fourth drink and, ashamed of his enjoyment of his own doubt, say to his mother as she bent over the steaming sink: "Come on, Mom, was it a Dodge or a Buick? You can at least tell me that much. What kind of car was Dad driving that day?"

During that period of time, because he needed to sit down and think things out, but could not make himself sit down and think things out, Murphy used his parents' house as a kind of retreat house. Small, white and neat, dominated by closets and furnace heat, it was a house in the confines of which he felt at once claustrophobic and clear-headed. About its place in his life there was something, he felt, both mystical and oppressive. Driving or riding home, sometimes in a car, sometimes in a bus or a train, he

felt that if he only knew what make of car his father had been
driving the day he'd been punched in the nose in front of precinct headquarters, he would then have *the answer*. What *the answer* was or even referred to, Murphy was uncertain sometimes
to the point of panic. But it had something to do with his parents' house, the way or mode by which he approached it.

Often Murphy approached it while drinking and once, trying
a combination of bus and train, he fell in with a drunken couple
from his hometown. The husband, red-headed and razor-thin,
was an upholsterer fresh out of the veterans hospital. Fat and
flirtatious, dim around the mouth, the wife was an acne-scarred
and squawlike woman in black slacks with hair parted and
combed, it looked to Murphy, with buffalo grease.

After buying his ticket Murphy had, like the drunken couple,
walked across the street for a drink. And like the drunken
couple, he watched the clock and left the tavern in plenty of time
to catch the bus. While they were walking across the street, however, the bus pulled away without them. If this upset Murphy, it
infuriated the red-headed upholsterer. After a long and loud
attack upon the ticket taker, he turned and grabbed Murphy by
the elbow. "Come on," he said, "we're taking a cab."

Murphy didn't like the way the upholsterer grabbed him by
the elbow and he didn't like the way the upholsterer sat him
down in the middle of the back seat between himself and his
wife, as if Murphy were somehow more with the upholsterer's
wife than the upholsterer was. But before he could do anything
about it, before he really *wanted* to do anything about it, they
were on the highway in the cab, the meter ticking too fast and
the upholsterer's wife sitting a little closer to Murphy than he
wanted her to sit. It was a gauzy August afternoon, the highway
a blue metallic corridor through high aggressive corn, and by

the time they passed the bus that should have taken them to the train, they were passing Murphy's half pint of rum back and forth among them.

When they got to the little town where the train would stop, the upholsterer did not, as he had said he would, "take care of the cab." In fact, he showed only enough money to pay three dollars of a nine-dollar fare. This did not surprise or anger Murphy, but it kept him from accompanying the upholsterer and his wife into the tavern with the Schlitz sign above its door. He was going to walk across the tracks, he told them, to see how late the train would be.

Two and a half hours, the lady stationmaster said. And that, she added, was at best a conservative estimate. For as long as he could, putting off the inevitable, Murphy sat around the little clapboard depot, walking out to stare down the heat-wavering, rust blue roadbed, finishing what little was left of the rum, turning to look across the tracks at the tavern with the Schlitz sign above its door. When an hour and a half had passed and the train was still at least an hour out of the station, Murphy went over there.

Sliding along the bar, slipping onto the first stool he saw, he ordered a double rum with a beer chaser. But when he dug into his pocket to pay for it, as if he had dug too roughly and touched off an alarm, a drunken voice roared, "I got that one, I got that one over here." The upholsterer, having found his money, greeted Murphy like a long lost friend. Throwing an arm around his shoulders, he walked him over to the table. There was country music on the jukebox and his wife was dancing not with one, but with two men. The fat one had a pipe clipped between his teeth, and the other one wore the empty cartridge belt of an iron worker. Both of them were grabbing and grinding at the upholsterer's wife, but the upholsterer wasn't mad at them, he was mad at the niggers. The first thing he said to Murphy was: "Right off now, don't think twice: are you a nigger lover?"

The Soybean Capital of the World

How Murphy could have known that that was the question the upholsterer was going to ask, how the gush of his greeting seemed to dictate that he ask just that, how the upholsterer's wife could have heard his words through the music from the dark end of the bar, Murphy did not know. But before he could answer, the upholsterer's wife was at the table and the upholsterer's question: *are you a nigger lover,* had set the tone for the afternoon.

What that tone was, Murphy could not quite say. But he knew that it would get him drunk and that it would get him home, it would take him edged, lurching and inquisitive to his parents' house, it would set him down finally in his mother's kitchen where, at about nine or ten P.M., in a voice lowered so that it would not wake his father, he would ask his mother once more about the Negro and the punch in the nose in front of precinct headquarters, and when she told him again that she didn't want to talk about it, Murphy would ask her whether it was a Dodge or Buick, to tell him at least what make of car his father had been driving that day.

That afternoon Murphy, the upholsterer and the upholsterer's wife did not take the train at all. They drove to Decatur, Illinois, Murphy's hometown, in a pickup truck to the bed of which had been bolted a Plexiglas camper. The camper carried on its sides faded decals of striking bass and pike and Murphy and the upholsterer rode in back, while the upholsterer's wife rode in front between the fat, pipe-smoking man, who drove, and the blunt blond man with the cartridge belt. The back of the camper was full of fishing tackle. There were rods and reels and bait boxes; there were bits of broken styrofoam and crumbling rolls of foam rubber. From its louvered windows, windows that were stuck shut and wouldn't open, from its banging gaffs and anchors, from its slimed stringers and fouled fishhooks hung an atmosphere so brutal and obvious, Murphy wondered if the upholsterer knew as certainly as he himself did, what the two men between whom she then rode were going to do to the upholsterer's wife, right there in the back of the camper, before very much longer, before certainly the afternoon was fully out.

If the upholsterer knew such a thing, it didn't for the time being at least, much bother or interest him. He was off once more on the niggers, happy to heap upon Murphy his tedium and toxicity, the booze mixing so thick with the bigotry, he seemed to be praying to the Negroes he sought to curse.

While the upholsterer sputtered and muttered, Murphy wondered how he had gotten himself where he had gotten himself that afternoon. But because it was an old question with Murphy, he had to force from his face the smile he wanted to smile as he sat in the back of an airless, cluttered, fish-rank camper with a red-headed, bigoted, alcoholic upholsterer whose wife was about again, not with one but a couple of men, to cuckold him.

Maybe it was the rum that had gotten him there, Murphy thought, or maybe it was the upholsterer's wife. If she was fat and baggy in the slacks, pitted, dim and otherwise oily, she was with the upholsterer, swift, curt, certain. When, dancing at the dark end of the bar, she'd heard the upholsterer ask if Murphy was a "nigger lover," she'd gotten to the table with an ease and speed that stunned Murphy, put him in a momentary awe of her.

She called the upholsterer Tilden. She said, "Are you off on that again, Tilden? Do we have to hear more on that subject, Tilden?" Then, though it had taken her awhile to do so, she had gotten the upholsterer off the subject of the niggers and the nigger lovers, onto the subject of the bus. The way the bus had pulled off without them. The upholsterer still couldn't get over it. He took Murphy's arm and he took his wife's hand. He leaned toward them. "We were there," he said, "five minutes early. All three of us were there five minutes early and they took off without us. They took off without us. The sons a bitches by god just took off without us."

In the upholsterer's fervor, in the grip of his grainy, red-haired hand, Murphy felt, he had to admit, a current, the electricity of an injustice the three of them had suffered together. Because it was heady and tawdry and would get him drunk, Murphy tried to resist it. But he couldn't. Along with the rum, it was there, the electricity and injustice of the bus having taken off, at least five minutes early, without them.

As the upholsterer squeezed his arm and talked about it, Murphy recalled the tavern across the street from the bus station, the way he, Murphy, ticket in hand, had left the tavern exactly eight minutes before the bus was to leave. Halfway across the street though, he'd heard a high-pitched, keening curse and looked up to see the upholsterer raise and shake his fist at a bus Murphy recognized immediately as *his* bus. It was a Greyhound and it was rounding the far corner of the station. The upholsterer didn't stop shaking his fist at it until, taking a right at a green light, it disappeared behind a billboard cut in the shape of an orange garbage truck across which was written: WE NEVER REFUSE REFUSE. By the time Murphy got to the ticket window, the upholsterer was already there, shaking two tickets at the ticket taker's face.

Pointing to a clock above the ticket taker's head, the upholsterer said: "What time does that clock say?"

"1:10 P.M."

"And what time was that bus supposed to leave?"

"1:15 P.M."

"So that bus took off early, right?"

Looking at the counter in front of him, the ticket taker clicked his ballpoint pen.

"That bus took off five minutes early, right?"

Again the ticket taker clicked his ballpoint pen and thrusting them even closer to the ticket taker's face, the upholsterer shook his tickets and said: "Now just what in the hell can I do with these? Could you tell me that? Just what in the hell can I do with these?"

As he listened to the ticket taker tell the upholsterer what he could do with his tickets, Murphy looked around the bus station. What he felt first and most was an embarrassment, a fear that someone might think that he, Murphy, was with the upholsterer and his wife, that they were a party, that they were a threesome. But when he saw that except for himself, the ticket taker, the upholsterer and the upholsterer's wife, the bus station was empty, his apprehension turned to anger. It was slow and secondhand, an anger the upholsterer owned most of, but Murphy was beginning to feel and share it too. The ticket taker was telling them about Indianapolis. He was giving them the address not of a bus station, but of a train station in Indianapolis, explaining that since what they had purchased was a train and not a bus ticket, that the bus only *took* them to the train, that he himself could not give them a refund, that they would have to mail their unused tickets to a train station in Indianapolis for a refund.

For awhile all the upholsterer seemed able to say was: "Refund? Refund? I don't want a goddamned refund! Screw Indianapolis, Indiana! I want to go to Decatur, Illinois!"

When Murphy heard the name of his own hometown spoken that way, when he heard the upholsterer say screw Indianapolis, Indiana, he wanted to go to Decatur, Illinois, when Murphy thought *so do I, so do I,* he felt a low dull thrill that pulled on him like booze, the dumb combustions and exaggerations of the rum he'd drunk in the tavern across the street. As the upholsterer began to shout that he not only *wanted* to go to Decatur, Illinois, but *had* to go to Decatur, Illinois, that they were *expecting* him in Decatur, Illinois, that he might have a *job* waiting for him in Decatur, Illinois, Murphy felt certain that he too had to get to Decatur, that there was something crucial and urgent about it, that if he didn't get there something awful might happen.

Though Murphy knew this was a lie, that he was slightly drunk and nothing awful would happen if he didn't get to Decatur, for the moment it didn't matter. Nor did it matter that there was no job waiting for the upholsterer in Decatur, that his only job was to get that afternoon as drunk or even drunker than he was acting now. The upholsterer stood in a shaft of bus station sunlight. Freckled and frail, made of blue bone, rust and dust motes, his hands flashed the tickets in front of the ticket taker's face. With each word he spoke, his voice became more shrill, strident, self-righteous. Everyone, even the ticket taker, seemed to sense that the upholsterer had never been this right before, would never be this right again.

By the time the bus station clock said 1:15 P.M., the ticket taker had produced two pre-addressed envelopes and had placed stamps on them. When he offered one to the upholsterer and one to Murphy, the upholsterer, as if the ticket taker had given him a cue to do so, raised his fist and said: "We don't want your goddamned stamped envelopes! We're going to Decatur, Illinois!"

It was then that he turned, grabbed Murphy by the elbow and said: "Come on we're taking a cab."

In the cab on the highway with the corn flashing past and the meter ticking much too fast, the upholsterer began immediately to crow and brag. But because Murphy himself wanted to crow and brag, to exaggerate and exalt the injustice of the bus having taken off five minutes early and without them, because flashing past the heavy, overbearing corn, gaining ground already on the bus that should have taken them to the train, they seemed to have just gotten away with something, not to have robbed the bus station or set fire to it, but something like that, because he knew such thoughts were nothing but the rum rumbling inside him, Murphy could no longer hide it from them, he had to offer the upholsterer and the upholsterer's wife a hit from his half pint of rum.

As soon as he did so, he knew that he had made a mistake. Thinking back on it, Murphy thought about her lips. The way the upholsterer's wife's lips touched the rim of his half pint of rum. Her mouth was dim and she looked like an Indian. When the upholsterer drank, his Adam's apple worked too hard. Under the thin skin of his throat, it looked somehow scientific, like a pink pump moving up and down, a syphon that would heighten the proof of the rum he was drinking. Watching it, Murphy thought, *I'm feeding firewater to Indians.*

Even as he thought the thought the upholsterer shouted, "Honk! Honk! Honk!"

At that moment, the cab was passing the bus that should have been taking them to the train and there was something ducklike and insane in the upholsterer's delight at its so doing. He grinned and shook his fist at the bus. He called the bus driver a son of a bitch and asked the cab driver again to honk! honk! honk!

Gripping both his knees, rocking back and forth as if to urge the cab on faster, the upholsterer began again to crow and brag about how he "told 'em" and "showed 'em" back at the bus station, going on and on until they'd arrived at the little town where the train would stop.

The depot was located at the junction of the Illinois Central and Norfolk and Western tracks. When a freight blew through, the whole place would shake. The concussion was so great, Murphy thought he could smell it, a mixture of sun, steel and creosote, a scent that went back to the nineteenth century. Also, compliments of the D.A.R., there was a flagpole, a stone and a bronze plaque with Lincoln's profile on it. At this junction, on February 11, 1861, Lincoln had made his farewell address to the people of Illinois. The plaque read: "I am leaving you on an errand of national importance, attended as you are aware with considerable difficulties. Let us believe as some poet has expressed it: behind the cloud the sun is still shining. I bid you affectionate farewell."

As he read, Murphy smiled. But it was a smile he couldn't sustain. At that moment the sun was not behind a cloud. It was beating into Murphy's brain. He turned from the plaque in sobering disgust.

It was then that he saw the bus driver and the bus. It was stopped at the bottom of a short flight of gray wooden stairs, the same color and blister of the depot. If its tires looked vaguely deflated, the bus itself looked bloated and overchromed, gave off an air of the stationary and the listless into which the bus driver himself seemed snugly to fit. He stood in the open door, half in shadow, half in light. His mouth held both a cigarette and toothpick. Though he was fat, his uniform was clean, sharply creased and his shoes were shined to a sparkle. With his hat tipped back, with blue smoke streaming from both his nostrils, with a neat gut hung over the big Greyhound buckle of his belt, he looked to Murphy like a frustrated cop or airplane pilot, an officious prick who liked nothing better than to leave people behind, to teach them the lesson of his own importance and punctuality.

What particularly burned Murphy, though, was the fact that the bus looked as empty as the depot did. Evidently, the bus driver had not only left early and without Murphy, the upholsterer and the upholsterer's wife, he had done so in an empty bus. About both his stance and his management of the cigarette and toothpick, there was a suggestion, too, that he had done this before, that he was a vicious and inveterate strander of travelers in taverns, taking off too early in empty buses for trains he knew would be late.

Though he couldn't remember doing so, though he was vaguely surprised to find it there, Murphy had gotten his ticket out of his pocket and was holding it in his hand. Looking at the bus, he began to think of it as *his* bus, like a car that had been stolen from him, one upon which he had stumbled, complete with its thief, long before the cops could. Tightening his grip on his ticket, finding in it a feel of keys or key rings, something that might vaguely weight and sharpen a punch, he wanted to walk up to the bus driver and punch him in the nose, drive the cigarette and toothpick right through to the other side of his head.

Instead, he turned and walked back toward the depot. After finishing what little was left of the rum, he stood for a long time and stared at the steel square where the Illinois Central crossed the N&W tracks. Drunkenly, telekinetically, he was trying to draw from the rails, spikes and ties, from the sunlight and the proximity of the Lincoln plaque, more strength and significance than were there. Murphy knew what he should do. He should walk over to the highway and hitchhike back into town. Once there, he should sit down and think out what he had to do. For a moment he picked up his duffel bag and wavered. When he did so, he felt something wobble and halt in the middle of his gut.

Putting down his duffel bag, he knew why he had been waiting around the depot as long as he had been. Partly it was a matter of sobering up, but more than that it was a matter of striking poses. At the intersection of the tracks, particularly when a freight blew through, Murphy felt photogenic and dramatic, a suntanned mustachioed young man traveling alone and light, going a lot farther than the forty-five miles to his parents' house in Decatur.

Below that, though, there was something even worse. He was waiting, Murphy knew, for the upholsterer and the upholsterer's wife. He wanted somehow to be wooed by them, to see them stagger across the tracks in his direction. The upholsterer would put a hand on his shoulder. Showing some cash, he'd ask Murphy to join them for a drink. Murphy of course would say no. But the upholsterer's wife would take his arm and coax him. Together the three of them would turn toward the tavern with the Schlitz sign above its door.

At this point (though Murphy couldn't explain quite why), the upholsterer would notice what he should have noticed before. Whispering *son of a bitch,* he'd try to break toward the bus driver and the bus. What would ensue would not even be a scuffle. Murphy would simply reach out, grab the upholsterer by the shirt and hold him until he calmed down.

When he felt the flimsy cotton of the upholsterer's white shirt balled and bound up in his fists, Murphy looked down at his hands. Again, they surprised him. Alone in front of the depot, he was standing with his hands closed very tightly, his knuckles showing white against a hurt that, again, slipped up on and shamed him. Unclenching his fists, Murphy knew that he not only wanted, but he had *expected*, he had been *waiting for*, the upholsterer and the upholsterer's wife to stagger across the tracks to ask him to join them for a drink in the tavern with the Schlitz sign above its door.

Below Murphy's feet, the concrete platform of the depot began to shake. Out of the west came the *blat, blat,* of an N&W freight. Murphy picked up his duffel bag, but he couldn't move. He knew what he should do. He should walk to the highway and hitchhike back into town. Alone in his room, he probably wouldn't come up with any answers. But getting there, deciding on his own to go there, would be an answer in itself.

Murphy couldn't turn and walk toward the highway though, and the freight seemed to help in his failure to do so. Waiting until the last possible moment, he ran across the tracks. Feeling under his feet and in his teeth the drone of the diesel engine, receiving against the entire left side of his body its double *blat* of warning, he headed for the tavern with the Schlitz sign above its door. Just before he stepped inside, he told himself a lie. He was not going to look for the upholsterer or the upholsterer's wife. In fact, he was going to try to avoid them. If they had a table and asked him to join them, he was going politely to say no. He was going to sit alone at the bar and have one drink. He was going to try to figure out what he had to do.

What he had to do, Murphy thought, was to get out of there and take a piss. But the camper was banging and clattering much too fast down a country road, kicking up a pale trail of dust that powdered the cornfields through which they seemed to be plowing. Sitting on a roll of foam rubber, Murphy wished he had a piss tube. Once when he was in the Marine Corps in southern California, they moved north to the High Sierras for snow exercises. They flew there in planes called "shivering shithouses." At about twelve thousand feet, everything began to shiver and shake, everybody had to urinate. Hooked to, but detachable from a stanchion in the middle of the cargo bay, was a piss tube, a rubber funnel to which was attached a thin, red rubber hose. About it there was a look of the catheter, as if when it began to climb, cool, shiver and shake, the plane itself had to urinate, and laughing and staggering with the piss tube in your hand and a long line behind you, you were simply helping it out, this heavy, two-tailed, diuretic, military bird, its urine falling like a fine yellow fog onto the High Sierras, the great green pine forests of northern California.

But Murphy wasn't sober in a plane above northern California, he was drunk in the back of an air-tight, fish-rank, eighty-mile-an-hour camper in central Illinois. Beside him, drunken, dithered, demented, the upholsterer held a Little League baseball bat. He was pretending it was a guitar. Fingering its handle, strumming it across the trademark, he sang:

> I'd walk a mile,
> Christ's mile,
> For my mommy and daddy.

Murphy wished he would stop. But he didn't want to ask him to, he didn't want to set him off. Since they'd gotten into the camper, since he'd found the baseball bat and picked it up, the upholsterer had been acting more and more crazy. Things had gotten crazy back in the tavern. First the upholsterer began to imply that he, not Murphy, had paid for most of the cab fare. When Murphy let him get away with that, he began to insinuate that the cab had been not his own, but Murphy's idea. Though he knew this was leading up to something, something he wasn't going to let the upholsterer get away with, Murphy could not remember when the upholsterer had first mentioned the camper, when the upholsterer had first grabbed his arm, motioned to the dark end of the bar and said: "They got a camper and they're going to Decatur." But he remembered that the idea of the camper frightened him, that his fright turned immediately to anger, then impatience and resolve. Murphy had shaken his head and said: "Nope. I'm taking the train." But the upholsterer wouldn't hear of it. Squeezing Murphy's arm a little tighter, leaning a little closer, he whispered: "We can get there faster in the camper."

When the upholsterer said that, Murphy felt a strange temptation. He wanted to throw his drink into the upholsterer's face. To do so would be, he knew, the liquid equivalent of a kiss or fist. Such knowledge came and went so quickly Murphy saw, for a second, his drink drip from the eyelashes and lips of the upholsterer. He blinked and it was as if someone else had seen what he'd just seen, the same imposter who had, a moment before, wanted to flick his drink into the upholsterer's face.

Ashamed of himself, Murphy stood up. At the dark end of the bar, tapping a foot to the music, pressed between the fat, pipe-smoking man and the blunt blond man with the cartridge belt, the upholsterer's wife punched buttons on the jukebox. When Murphy passed her, she looked up at him and winked.

In the toilet, swaying as he moved toward it, Murphy wanted in a vague way to test his fist on the wall above the urinal. A second inscription, printed there not in bronze but in large, neat, black Magic Marker kept him from doing so.

If your hose is short
Or your pump is weak,
Step up close
Or you'll piss on your feet.

Piss on their feet and piss on their plot. But piss most of all, Murphy
thought, *upon the buttons the lady's now punching.* Standing at the
urinal, Murphy could feel the upholsterer's wife on the other
side of the wall punching buttons, feeding into the jukebox a
program or plan for the ride to Decatur.

Zipping up, Murphy knew, long before he ever saw it or got
into it, that the camper would be owned and driven by the fat,
pipe-smoking man, that he would drive too fast down powder-
white country roads, that the upholsterer's wife would ride up
front between the fat, pipe-smoking man and the blunt blond
man with the cartridge belt, that the camper itself would be a
homemade, jerryrigged thing with a broken back door that only
bolted closed from the outside, that he, Murphy, would be
locked into the back of it with the upholsterer, that the blunt
blond man with the cartridge belt would do the locking in, that
when he boarded behind the upholsterer, Murphy would notice
for the first time a heavy, empty leather sheath on the cartridge
belt, one that looked less like a sheath than a holster, something
that might hold not the tools of an iron worker, but a Colt .45,
the kind of pistol a guard might carry, that when he thought that
thought and the door slammed shut and locked behind him, the
camper would seem less like a camper than a Black Maria from
some mental institution, one to which, for dementia praecox and
dire dipsomania, both he and the upholsterer were being taken.

Such thoughts took Murphy first to the bar, then toward the
door. When, halfway there, the upholsterer caught him by the
arm and asked him where he was going, Murphy turned and
told him that he was going to catch the train.

It was as if, in saying what he'd said, he had called for the train and it had come. Out of Detroit, the diesel had a dirty, dogged, soot-blue, Great Lakes look to it. Keeping an eye on its revolving headlight, Murphy, duffel bag in hand, a fresh half pint of rum on his hip, had plenty of time to saunter across the tracks. He didn't have to rush at all. The upholsterer did though.

Standing on the depot platform, Murphy focused on the upholsterer's feet. Shod in paint-spattered, thin-toed, black business shoes, they looked like feet the upholsterer had many times pissed upon. The cuffs of his pants, too, looked wet, wide and heavy, as if the urine in them might stiffen and trip the upholsterer, send him sprawling into the greasy wheels of the diesel.

When it gave out its double *blat* of admonition, Murphy heard a horn within a horn. If he had been warned, so had the upholsterer. But the upholsterer paid no heed. Already he had crossed the last set of tracks and was on the depot platform. Grabbing Murphy by the arm, he told him not to waste his money, not to take the train. Pulling two crumpled tickets from his pocket, he spoke the word he so disdained back at the bus station, reminded Murphy they could get a *refund* on their tickets, could get back the money they'd spent on the cab.

Half drunk, Murphy gripped his own ticket and knew the upholsterer knew that neither of them would ever mail their tickets to a train station in Indianapolis for a refund, that the only way he could waste the money he had spent on it was *not* to use his ticket, was *not* to shrug the upholsterer's hand off his arm and board the train.

Yet he did not move. Like the upholsterer's insinuation that he, not Murphy, had paid for the cab, that the cab itself had somehow been more Murphy's idea than his own, the suggestion that they could now save and return their tickets for a refund seemed so drunk, remote and refutable, so ominous and easy to ignore, Murphy could not ignore it: he saw once more the upholsterer's drunken dash after him across the tracks.

45

❖   ❖   ❖

Across the back bumper of the camper, in large black letters, a sign had been stenciled. It read: WARNING THIS VEHICLE STOPS AT ALL BARS. It didn't though. Nor did it stop at railroad crossings. The thought, sight and sound of the railroad crossing to which the camper had raced the train made Murphy sick. A nausea of bigotry and cigarettes, it began when, walking the length of the depot platform, listening to the upholsterer call the train "nothing but a nigger train," they staggered down the steps past the bus driver and the bus. Murphy no longer wanted any cursing, any confrontation. But he expected the upholsterer at least to notice the bus driver and the bus. When he did not, when he passed both as if they no longer mattered, the upholsterer's drunkenness seemed to weight and darken the regard in which the bus driver held them. He still stood fat and neat in the opened door, blue cigarette smoke still poured from both his nostrils. About the dual-exhaust density and volume of the smoke, about Murphy's sense that it need never thin nor stop, there was a quality of the pet cock, boiler, burst radiator, a hint of the steaming, whistling, metal wreck a train might make of a camper.

As soon as they were locked inside, the upholsterer announced that they were going to "beat that nigger train to Decatur." In order to do so, Murphy knew, they would have to beat it to a crossing about five miles out of town. Evidently the upholsterer had extracted from the fat, pipe-smoking man a promise to try just that. When the warning bells and lights stopped and it rose in front of them, the black-and-white-striped barrier arm seemed to work like a starting gate. The train had pulled away only a few moments before, but they shot across the tracks after it. To get to the narrow, chuckholed blacktop that would put them parallel to it, they had to pass through the shadow of a huge, gray-blue grain elevator. A place of scales and scrutiny, of

CUSTOM GRINDING AND SEED CLEANING, a place where farmers in trucks and tractors did a lot of lining up and waiting, the grain elevator was fronted along its entire length by taverns. Each one made of the fat, pipe-smoking man, a liar. Murphy kept count and they passed one-two-three-four bars before they passed out of the shadow of the grain elevator. But their vehicle stopped at none. Four bars, no stops. The thought refused to stop. Like a calliope stuck on a single, shrill, steaming note, the memory and tempo of the four passed taverns kept Murphy counting. He was on his fifty-sixth telephone pole when the upholsterer jabbed him in the ribs with his Little League baseball bat. "Look at the niggers," he shouted, "look at the niggers!"

Murphy looked at the train and it was true. In all of its windows, dank, greenish windows that suggested faulty ventilation, the heads of elderly black ladies appeared. Bound not for glory, but at the end of its run for St. Louis, Missouri, the train was without question a Negro train. This made Murphy fear it and want to be aboard it all the more.

Shaking his Little League baseball bat, the upholsterer roared, "Pass the black bastards, pass the black bastards!" Watching him, Murphy saw the resemblance that all along he'd barely been missing. The upholsterer looked like Red Schoendienst, former manager of the St. Louis Cardinals. Thinking of cardinals, how often on birdseed bags, road maps and baseball caps they were stitched, printed, misrepresented, the harsh red of their bodies, the bright yammering yellow of their beaks, Murphy thought he saw inside his pink profile the size and shape of the upholsterer's brain. He was a birdbrain and Murphy knew what he had in mind: just as the cab had passed the bus that should have taken them to the train, so the camper would pass the train that should have taken them to Decatur.

It seemed to be trying to do just that. As they edged alongside the locomotive, the upholsterer screamed as he had screamed before, "Honk! Honk! Honk!" Again, there was something ducklike and insane in the sound he made, as if it should have come not from a man but a goose, not from a mouth but a bill. In a panic of claustrophobia and condescension, Murphy was certain that he was going to be killed.

Sitting with his back to the action, he dreamed of a secret hand brake buried in the underbody of the camper. When he reached through the foam rubber and found it, when he pulled up on it, all four wheels would lock in a long, flame-framed stop. In the absence of such a hand brake, Murphy gripped the ticket in his pocket. In the wilt and grit of it, he felt a finality: to hold a ticket for a train you were trying to pass, he thought, was to hold a ticket for a train that would kill you. It was a detail, an irony and paradox over which the investigating cops would be unable to get. When they found that between the two of them, Murphy and the upholsterer held three tickets for the train that killed them, they would shake their heads and blow blue cigarette smoke from their nostrils; they would remark upon it so often and long, the fact of the unused train tickets might find its way into the report of the wreck in the newspaper. To accompany a photograph of blowtorches and corn tassles, the flattened camper thrown into a cornfield, welders in helmets working to free the bodies trapped inside it, Murphy composed a caption: DUO HOLDS TICKETS FOR TRAIN THAT KILLS THEM. When Murphy thought the word *duo,* he thought the word *duet.* Gripped in grim duet, he and the upholsterer screamed, "Honk! Honk! Honk!"

Even as Murphy felt that sound form in his tight-shut mouth, he felt that he was not going home, not going to Decatur, Illinois, he was going crazy. Against a jangling of warning bells, a blink and flicker of warning lights, he whispered: *This is the way to get there, this is the way to get there.* When the upholsterer screamed, "Hot damn," Murphy closed his eyes and waited for a collision that did not come.

What came instead was Giotto. For a long time Murphy couldn't get Giotto off his mind. Specifically, Giotto's *Kiss of Judas.* Rattling along in the back of the fish-rank camper, looking at the upholsterer's pink profile, Murphy saw Giotto's Judas in profile, eyes asquint and lips apucker, an arm thrown heavily around Christ's shoulder. Beside and behind him, two of Pilate's men had closed in so tight, Judas' nose and lips seemed to appear in triplicate, as if when he got it Christ was going to get it not once but thrice. Under a halo like a helmet, Christ was looking Judas square in the eye. You couldn't see it, but Murphy liked to think that someplace below where the painting stopped, Giotto's Christ had a fist cocked, was going, when their lips met, to blast Judas in the mouth.

At the moment, the upholsterer's mouth seemed to test anew Murphy's determination not to hit, kiss or spit some rum at it. Sitting on his roll of foam rubber, watching him strum the trademark of his Little League baseball bat, Murphy could believe neither the song the upholsterer had chosen to sing, nor the voice in which he sang it. High pitched, nasal and countrified, his voice, without any help from the camper, seemed to lift, kick and swirl the dust of the country roads down which they were now driving. Over and over he sang:

> I'd walk a mile,
> Christ's mile,
> For my mommy and daddy.

Listening to him, Murphy wanted to bang on the dim double window that separated him and the upholsterer from the three who rode up front. Somehow he would get them to stop and let him out. When they did so, he would make his way back to the tracks. Walking alone to Decatur, counting the miles and the railroad ties between "here" and his parents' house in Decatur, he'd come up with "the answer."

Because he suspected that "the answer" would be simply "Dodge" or "Buick," would name nothing more or less than the make of the car they were driving the day his father had been punched in the nose by a Negro, Murphy was certain that if he heard it even one more time, the upholsterer's song would burst his bladder.

It was as if someone up front shared his trouble. To a clatter of gaffs and anchors, they swung off the country road onto a blacktop. Within seconds they had stopped in front of a tavern. When the door of the camper opened, the upholsterer's wife was standing there waiting.

Taking the upholsterer by the elbow, she walked him across the road. They stood against a grain elevator. Behind and around them, in a mineral glint of corn, soybeans and gravel, pigeons strode and pecked. In the shadows by the scales there were shovels worn silver from scooping. Murphy tried not to do so, but he thought about a fight, that the upholsterer might take a punch at his wife. On the hot green indoor-outdoor carpeting of the tavern steps, the blunt blond man had stopped and was watching too.

Murphy couldn't hear much of what the upholsterer's wife was saying. But she was saying it hard, with an urgency that seemed to Murphy urinary, that made him suspect she was the one who had called for the stop they had made. She still held the upholsterer's elbow. Murphy was certain he heard the name "Tilden" a number of times, and once or twice "that song." Then raising a finger and shaking it, the upholsterer's wife seemed to shake the pigeons loose. Against a green sheen and batter of wings, Murphy thought he heard the upholsterer say "Shit." But by the time they had recrossed the road, it was clear what his wife's words had meant. The upholsterer could enter the tavern and use its toilet, but he could neither drink nor stay.

About the upholsterer's acceptance of the law his wife laid down, about the blunt blond man's enforcement of it, there was something so solemn and tacit, Murphy got the impression they had done this together before. When the upholsterer emerged from the door marked MEN, the blunt blond man got up from the table and followed him. With his head bowed, with his paint-spattered shoes in a shuffle, the upholsterer might have been a prisoner; with his cartridge belt, with his dignity and deference, the blunt blond man might have been his guard or, if they were in the Marine Corps, his chaser.

Thinking of shotguns, Colt .45s and chasers, of ice plant, rattlesnakes and prisoners with white bull's-eyes stenciled on the backs of their utility jackets, Murphy ordered a shot of 150-proof rum with a malt liquor chaser. Outside in the sunlight, the blunt blond man was locking the upholsterer into the back of the camper. When he slapped the upholsterer on the shoulder, Murphy turned and walked toward the toilet.

They seemed not to follow a route but a cool porcelain trail of troughs, toilets and urinals to Decatur. Each time he stood in front of one of them, Murphy thought about making a break for it. Something about the darkness of the hallway down which he'd just walked, the dim red EXIT sign at the end of it, urged escape. But Murphy made no escapes, no getaways. Standing at the bars of taverns in the little corn and soybean towns that took them closer and closer to Decatur, he thought dimly of the grain elevators across the road, the tracks beyond. If he slipped out the back door, if he looped past the filling station turned beauty parlor, if he noted the clash of the defunct pumps with the wigs in the window, if he walked the N&W roadbed to Decatur, would he need a piece of paper and a pencil to tote the railroad ties? Though it never quite struck him as funny, the more Murphy thought about it, the more laughable it became.

Also, as he came to like the wife and her escorts less and less, he came to pity the upholsterer more and more. He began to think of him as "that poor son of a bitch locked out there in the camper." This lent to Murphy's drinking a high, light loyalty and hurry that sent him again and again outside to unlock the back of the camper, to give the upholsterer a little air, to keep him company.

The upholsterer wasn't much company. He kept telling Murphy the story of his life. The first time he heard the story of the upholsterer's life, Murphy was not surprised that he had heard it all before, but he felt somehow that he *ought* to be surprised that he had heard it all before, that he somehow owed it to the upholsterer to be surprised that he had heard it all before. Each time the upholsterer took Murphy by the arm and told him he was going to tell him something that he had never told anybody else before, Murphy knew that the upholsterer was going to tell him that he was an alcoholic. He had already told him two or three times in the tavern with the Schlitz sign above its door. Yet each time he squeezed Murphy's elbow and told him he was going to tell him something that he had never told anybody else before, the upholsterer did so in a hushed, halting, confidential way that seemed each time to test just a little more stringently Murphy's determination not to hit, kiss or spit some rum into his face.

Sitting on his roll of foam rubber, Murphy could feel the blunt blond man up front smiling at him. The upholsterer was frowning at him. He was saying, "Look, I'm going to tell you something I never told anybody else before."

But before he could begin again to confess that he was an alcoholic, that he was a man with "no personal control" over the stuff at all, that the stuff was "just like poison" to him, Murphy saw what he'd been looking for, the big black-and-white billboard with the gold gilt lettering that read:

WELCOME TO

DECATUR, ILLINOIS

THE SOYBEAN CAPITAL OF THE WORLD

Pointing at it, Murphy said, "Did you know that?"

"Did I know what?"

"That Decatur, Illinois, is the Soybean Capital of the World."

"Yeh," the upholsterer said, "I knew that."

For a moment there was silence. In it Murphy felt what he always felt about Decatur, Illinois, his own hometown, being the Soybean Capital of the World. He felt a profound and humorless confusion. Many times Murphy had tried to laugh about it, had tried to make a joke out of Decatur, Illinois, his own hometown, being the Soybean Capital of the World. But it never worked. In order for it to be funny or odd or ridiculous that Decatur, Illinois, claimed to be the Soybean Capital of the World, you had to be at least five hundred miles away from Decatur, Illinois, you had to have a Great Lake or a plains state or two, maybe a mountain range or the Texas panhandle between you and Decatur, Illinois. More and more Murphy had none of them.

So he'd had to stop trying to make a joke out of Decatur, Illinois, being the Soybean Capital of the World. Still, as the camper clattered and rattled past the billboard proclaiming it to be just that, as Murphy managed to glimpse the reverse side, the plain black lettering that read:

HURRY BACK TO

DECATUR, ILLINOIS

THE SOYBEAN CAPITAL OF THE WORLD

he couldn't help but shake his head. Somehow, without coming out and saying so, the sign implied that in Decatur, Illinois, if you looked hard enough, you could find some kind of soybean center or concession, a place where you could *do* something with

soybeans, maybe bathe in or gaze at them, a soybean hot springs
or house of horrors to which, if you weren't careful, you would
be brought in a camper against your will.

The upholsterer was still claiming what he'd already claimed
before, that he had never had D.T.'s. All the nurses and the
doctors back at the V.A. hospital thought that he was going to
have D.T.'s, they were set and ready for him to have D.T.'s, they
even *bet* each other that he'd have D.T.'s, but he didn't, he "fooled
'em," he'd never once in his life, he told Murphy, had *by god*
D.T.'s.

Then, as if to congratulate himself for never having had D.T.'s,
or maybe just to try to achieve once and for all what he had never
in his life achieved before, the snake-shaking, wing-battering,
feather-scattering delirium tremens, the upholsterer asked again
for a hit from the new half pint of rum Murphy carried on
his hip.

Murphy took it from his pocket. He held it, he stared at it.
From the time he bought it, he had felt indemnified by it. Each
time the upholsterer asked for a hit from it, Murphy's demur-
ring seemed to double and triple that indemnity. The half pint's
unbroken seal, its unshattered serial number worked in Murphy's mind like an insurance policy; to save the rum until they
got to Decatur, would get them safely to Decatur.

Now, however, they were safely in Decatur and the upholsterer
was smiling at him. It was a smile of collusion, collaboration.
Murphy could not remember exactly when it happened, but outside one of the little corn and soybean taverns at which they'd
stopped, the upholsterer's wife had popped her head into the
back of the camper. Pointing a finger at the bottle Murphy carried on his hip, she'd said, "Whatever you do don't give him any
of that shit." Then she'd slammed the door upon a maxim male
and muddled: because she was a woman and had forbidden him
to do so, sooner or later Murphy would have to give the upholsterer a hit from his half pint of rum.

Still, he didn't want to. He wanted to say *wait until we hit the beltline or this next stop sign, wait until the top of the viaduct, or wait until we get uptown.* If he let them, though, Murphy knew his reservations wouldn't stop. He wanted to save the seal and serial number on his half pint of rum not only until they'd gotten uptown and the upholsterer's wife had given them the slip, but until he himself had given the upholsterer the slip, left an extra five-dollar bill with the bartender and staggered out the back door while the upholsterer was taking a piss. If he could get that far without breaking them, he might save the seal and serial number on his half pint of rum not only until he got in and out of his parents' house, but in and out of Decatur itself, back to his room where he could erase with days of sobriety the dumb drama in which his dipsomania once more had placed him.

He didn't want to use a fingernail, he wanted to twist the cap off with the strength of his grip alone. That was what Murphy was trying to do when he saw the second sign, the one that read:

AVOID THE HEARSE
SAFETY FIRST

He always saw it from the top of the viaduct. Starched, scorched and strewn with soybeans, the viaduct passed through the middle of a huge soybean-processing plant. Murphy could never figure out why so many people got killed or maimed processing soybeans. But they did. Every year there were nine or ten soybean-processing deaths or maimings. He was musing over the curiosity of this, trying to fix in his mind what it would be like to die a death by soybeans, when he felt the train. He could not see it, but he could hear it and he could feel it. Plowing through the same cloud of yellow soybean smoke through which they were now plowing, it rattled and clacked on the tracks below them. Outside fog lights were blinking yellow against swirls of yellow soybean smoke and Murphy's reckoning was a dead one:

if they hadn't passed over it, he knew, they would have hit the train or the train would have hit them.

Beside him, the upholsterer was taking a long hit from the half pint of rum. Murphy knew neither how he had gotten the bottle nor how he had removed its cap. He knew one thing though. At the precise moment when he was least wondering why the upholsterer carried a knife, when he was farther perhaps than he had ever been in his life from wondering why the upholsterer carried a knife, the upholsterer wiped the back of his hand across his mouth and said to Murphy: "And then you wonder why I carry a knife."

Because he was so certain that the upholsterer's statement came first and his own wonder second, because he was absolutely sure that he hadn't gotten the order of things reversed, that he had *never once in his life* wondered why the upholsterer carried a knife, it frightened Murphy that the upholsterer carried a knife.

Murphy heard himself say: "You carry a knife?"

Then he heard the upholsterer say, "Sure I carry a knife. You ever hear of a upholsterer that *didn't* carry a knife?"

For a long time, Murphy tried to remember if he had ever heard of an upholsterer who didn't carry a knife. After awhile, however, the question of whether or not he had ever heard of an upholsterer who didn't carry a knife got lost in thoughts of upholstery itself. Murphy had sometimes wondered about it but had never understood it. When, for instance, he had to search behind the cushions of a sofa for coins or keys, he'd find crannies and crooks so deep and complex he was always afraid he'd cut himself. In his fingertips he'd feel a fear of foreign matter, of razor-sharp remnants some angry, hungover, hurried upholsterer had had to leave inside the sofa he'd been upholstering. Murphy had a memory of someone cutting himself that way. Because he thought he *ought* to think that someone was his father, he turned toward the upholsterer and said with more edge than he wanted to, "Pass the fucking rum."

As he drank, Murphy tried to do so, but couldn't stop thinking about upholstery. A craft of impasse, an art of hard-to-get-places, its practice, Murphy thought, might drive a man to drink. In his teeth, an upholsterer would carry a taste of tacks. In his hand he'd hold a tiny tack hammer. Often, the tips of his fingers would bleed and he'd tug on your sleeve, asking for more rum.

Twice Murphy and the upholsterer exchanged the half pint. On his third turn, Murphy killed it. Because he had a feeling that the upholsterer was looking at him, he looked at the floor. He stared at a jar he had stared at many times before. Like the billboard that proclaimed Decatur, Illinois, to be the Soybean Capital of the World, its label held words at which he could no longer afford to smile. It read:

TO

KEEP ME HOT

KEEP ME COLD

Rusty, crusted, lidless, the jar had once held horseradish made by one Dixie Rogers of Taylorville, Illinois. Dreaming not of a hand brake, but of a telephone buried deep in the underbody of the camper, Murphy thought about calling Dixie Rogers long distance in Taylorville, Illinois. If he got his party, he would ask how those words

TO

KEEP ME HOT

KEEP ME COLD

applied to the chill and plain craziness he felt at having first withheld then fed the upholsterer so much rum. If Dixie Rogers didn't understand, if Dixie Rogers didn't even answer, if from the other end of the line Murphy got nothing but silence, he might have to lighten up a little on his question. He might simply say: "Listen, Dixie, are you a man or are you a woman? That's all

I want to know. Dixie Rogers of Taylorville, Illinois, are you a boy or a girl?" Then with a grunt, he would slam the phone down on Dixie Rogers' ear.

The upholsterer seemed to have moved a little nearer. He had his hand on Murphy's arm again.

"Listen," he said, "I want to ask you a question."

When Murphy neither looked up nor answered, the upholsterer said, "Have you ever put somebody out?"

"What do you mean have I ever put somebody out?"

"You know," the upholsterer said and passed a frail, freckled fist in front of Murphy's face. "*With one punch.* Have you ever put somebody out *with one punch?*"

"I don't know," Murphy lied, "I might have."

The upholsterer was sitting very close to Murphy now. Sticking a bony finger into Murphy's ribs, he said, "How about me? Do you think you could put *me* out with one punch?"

Though Murphy felt the finger, he neither moved nor answered.

"Answer me," the upholsterer said and poked Murphy a little harder in the ribs. "Do you think you could put *me* out with one punch?"

"Look," Murphy said. "I don't think that's ever going to come up."

"No, I know," the upholsterer said. "But I've got to know, if you *had to,* could you put *me* out with one punch?"

Murphy turned to the upholsterer. Pale, powdered down with tavern talc, cigarette grit, he looked like a toilet tussler, a piss-trough pugilist. In drinking the rum, he seemed to have suffered an even greater loss of weight. If there was one man in the world he could put out with a single punch, Murphy thought, that man would be the upholsterer. Like the claw of a chicken, his finger still scratched Murphy's ribs. Brushing it off, Murphy thought if he ever *did* hit the upholsterer, if he ever caught him just so with, say, a right hook to the head, there would be no crunch or thud, but a bursting of white chicken feathers instead, a slow drift of the upholsterer from the living to the dead.

Fighting an excitement, a buzz in the hair on the back of his neck, Murphy said, "I don't know whether I could put you out with one punch or not."

"Well," the upholsterer smiled and shook his head. "I *hope* you can. I just *hope* you can. But if you ever have to, buddy boy, watch out. Because I'm a upholsterer and I carry a knife. Don't ever forget *I carry a knife*."

It was not a pocketknife, nor was it a knife with which one could practice upholstery. It was a switchblade. Even in the louvered, grimy light of the camper, it flashed and flickered. The upholsterer had produced it, blade and all, with a speed and snap that surprised and frightened Murphy. The Little League baseball bat was propped against the door of the camper. It had a close-quarters, clublike look that appealed to Murphy. For a moment, he tried to figure out how quickly he could get to it. Then he thought he'd simply ask the upholsterer to put the switchblade away. Before he could seriously consider doing either, however, the switchblade was gone and the upholsterer was patting his pants pocket. "I don't ever want to have to use this," he said, "on you or anybody else. But if I ever have to, buddy boy, don't forget I got my knife *right here in my pocket*."

There is, in the northeast end of Decatur, Illinois, a pocket of white poverty known locally as Dogpatch. That was where, when he looked out the window, Murphy found himself.

A semirural place of mailboxes, snuff and sunflowers, of Red Man Chewing Tobacco and tarpaper shacks set down on long, narrow lots the straw and cinder limits of which hold stoves, refrigerators and cars set up on blocks, Dogpatch is bound on all sides by railroad tracks and soybean-processing plants. Often Murphy had heard its inhabitants referred to as "yellow-

hammers." Loose limbed and light skinned, they were orthoped-
ically and orthodontically afflicted families said to engage in in-
cest. It was a myth that fascinated Murphy. Along with it went
the gang-bang. The girls of Dogpatch were said not only to accept their fathers and brothers, but to fuck indiscriminately and
sometimes in numbers. Another term for gang-bang was "pull a
train." That was the term Murphy preferred. Somewhere, sometime, he had seen a photograph of Charles Atlas pulling a train.
He was rigged up in a kind of harness and was straining migh-
tily. Yoked to the locomotives of the N&W and the Illinois Central, the pale daughters of Dogpatch would strain, Murphy
knew, even harder than Charles Atlas. He was thinking of bare
feet and cotton print dresses, of flour sack aprons and the back-
seats of cars set up on blocks, when the upholsterer began to
bang on the dim double window that separated them from the
three who rode up front.

What the upholsterer said, what he shouted over and over
again so clearly read Murphy's mind that both during and after
the shouting and the banging on the window, Murphy refused
not so much to believe what the upholsterer said, but the un-
canny timing with which he said it.

Grabbing Murphy's arm, the upholsterer shouted: "Look,
look, they got their hands between her legs! Both of them got
their hands between her legs!"

Murphy neither turned nor looked. He was thinking about
the upholsterer's switchblade knife. He was thinking that if he
did turn and confirm what the two men who rode up front were
doing to the upholsterer's wife, the upholsterer might turn on
him with his switchblade knife. It seemed to Murphy that he was
right. The upholsterer tugged so hard on his arm, he told him
to "look, look, look," with such fervor, Murphy got the impression that it was far more important to the upholsterer that he
turn and look than it was for the two men up front to stop doing
what they were doing to his wife.

After awhile the upholsterer stopped tugging and dug a finger into Murphy's ribs. "Did you see that," he said. "Did you see what those two sons of bitches were doing to my wife?"

When Murphy neither nodded nor shook his head, the upholsterer said: "Well *I* saw it, *I* saw it by god."

But in his voice there was a note both of doubt and dismissal: because Murphy hadn't turned and seen them do so, it didn't matter quite as much as it might have that the two men who rode up front had put their hands between his wife's legs.

The upholsterer had his hands clasped between his legs. He was rocking back and forth again. On the strength of that motion alone, after a moment or two of muttering, he managed to turn his attention from his wife to his car. That was why, it seemed, they had come to Dogpatch in the first place. So the upholsterer's wife could get the upholsterer's car.

She was unable to get the upholsterer's car. During her entire attempt to do so, Murphy remained locked in the back of the camper with the upholsterer. The upholsterer was raving. They were parked alongside his father's house. Across the street, a Roto-Rooter truck was working. Through the fish stench came soybean scorch and the trouble was with money. Who owed who a hundred and twenty-five dollars and twenty-four goddamned cents. Murphy could not and did not want to make any sense of it. At one point, he heard the upholsterer's wife speak the upholsterer's father's name. At that moment, though Murphy did not know exactly why, he wanted very much *not* to know the upholsterer's father's name. But he heard it anyway. Through the locked door of the camper he heard the upholsterer's wife say: "Owen says you owe him for a new carburetor."

Even before he grabbed him, Murphy knew the upholsterer was going to do so. Squeezing Murphy's elbow, the upholsterer said: "*New?* That carburetor's not *new.* I *rebuilt* that carburetor and you know how I can prove it to you?"

When Murphy neither looked at him nor answered, the upholsterer pushed his face even closer to Murphy's and said: "I can prove it to you because I scratched my initials in the side of the son of a bitch, that's how I can prove it to you!"

Again, because the upholsterer's focus seemed to switch so quickly, because he seemed to want to prove the truth of the rebuilt carburetor not to his wife or his father, but to him alone, Murphy was expecting the knife, a display of the switchblade knife with which he had scratched his initials into the side of the rebuilt carburetor. If he got it, Murphy thought, if anybody waved any switchblade knife in front of his face, he was going after the Little League baseball bat. But the upholsterer neither patted his pants pocket nor pulled his switchblade knife.

Before Murphy knew it, to the slam of a screen, then a camper door, they were backed out of there and the upholsterer had moved back to his side of the camper. He look dazed, spent. The rum and shouting had sent a sheen of grease across his face and for a long time he was quiet.

They seemed to take a different and a longer way out of Dogpatch than they had taken in. Mostly Murphy kept his eyes to the floor of the camper. But when at one point he did look up and out its window, he saw a strange sight.

The camper was moving slowly and the sun was very bright. Set against the front of a swaybacked little shack, stood a line of five sunflower plants. They were all between seven and eight feet tall and over the heads of each one of them a brown paper sack had been placed and tied down with a string. The sunflower plants looked droopy and desolate, but they were aligned in a more or less military way that made them look, Murphy thought, like five sunflower spies or assassins waiting for a sunflower execution squad to march up and blow their heads off.

On the pretext that the upholsterer himself had gotten too drunk to do so, that he would just foul things up if he came along, the upholsterer's wife went off in the camper to see about the apocryphal job, the one Murphy knew was not then and never had been awaiting the upholsterer in Decatur. Just before she left, she pointed a finger vaguely northeast and skyward, as if it were in that direction that the upholsterer's future lay. Murphy looked at it and figured that if the upholsterer followed the trajectory his wife's finger suggested, he would wind up working on sofas in a soybean-processing plant. It would be both a dangerous and an odd job, one at which a man might very easily lose an arm, a leg, even his life.

The upholsterer had agreed so readily with his wife that Murphy himself was determined not to do so: because she had given the upholsterer the slip, because Murphy knew she assumed that he in turn would give the upholsterer the slip, Murphy was stuck with him, he could not and would not give the upholsterer the slip. In bar after bar, thinking of upholsterers and slips, he looked up to see drink after drink drip from the eyelashes and lips of the upholsterer. Yet the temptation to hit, kiss or flick his drink into the upholsterer's face had grown so old and strong, he had withstood it so often and long, Murphy felt of all the men in all the bars through which they'd passed he was the least likely to hit, kiss or flick his drink into the face of the man standing next to him.

The upholsterer was standing next to him. He had his hand on Murphy's shoulder again and was telling him once more about Decatur. He was saying: "You say you know Decatur. You say you were borned and raised in Decatur, but you don't know Decatur. You don't really know this town. If you really want to know this town, you'll let me teach you a thing or two about this town."

When Murphy told the upholsterer that he didn't want to be taught a thing or two about this town, that he already knew as much about Decatur as he wanted to know about Decatur, the upholsterer said: "*OK, OK*. If you really want me to, I think I just *might* be able to teach you a thing or two about this town."

The first thing the upholsterer wanted to teach Murphy about

Decatur was the levee. He wanted to take Murphy to the levee.
When Murphy told the upholsterer that he'd already been to the
levee, that he already knew where the levee was, the upholsterer
said: "*OK, OK*. If you really want me to show you the levee, I'll
take you to the goddamned levee."

The upholsterer could not find the levee. Though the levee
runs roughly parallel to the N&W tracks and is located along a
stretch of three or four short, bar-crowded blocks, the upholsterer could not find the levee. They were on the levee all right
and Murphy knew it. But the upholsterer would not or could not
admit it. In every bar in which they stopped, the upholsterer
would order a vodka and Squirt. Before he drank it, however,
he'd sniff his glass and say to Murphy: "This ain't the levee. This
place ain't the goddamned levee."

But the upholsterer must have said more than that and he
must have said it louder than Murphy thought, because bartenders kept coming up and telling the upholsterer to watch his language, there were ladies present.

There were, in fact, ladies present. In bars all along the levee
there were large ladies sitting alone in booths. There was something, Murphy thought, Alaskan in their size and silence. Looking at them, he thought of sea lions and starch drivers. Murphy
did not know what a starch driver was. Through a cloud of yellow soybean smoke he had once seen STARCH DRIVER stenciled
on the side of a building in a soybean-processing plant. Looking
at the large ladies sitting alone in their booths he thought,
though, that they just might be starch drivers. Murphy knew he
was drunk, but still he wanted very badly to walk over to one of
the large ladies and ask her if she was a starch driver on her day
off or if starch driving was hard work or how much starch she'd
say she'd drive on an average shift. Murphy knew better, however, than to approach them. The upholsterer, though, did not.
He couldn't seem to stay away from them. In every bar in which
they stopped, he'd walk over to one of the large ladies and place

his hand on the booth behind her neck. Then he'd bend down toward her and pointing a finger at Murphy, he'd say: "Lady, tell this man over here this ain't the levee. Tell him this place ain't the goddamned levee."

The large ladies would neither look up nor answer. The bartenders would though. They'd come over and tell the upholsterer to leave the lady alone. If he couldn't leave the lady alone, he'd just have to drink up and leave.

Outside on the street, having drunk up and left, the upholsterer would shake his fist at the door of the bar from which he'd just been ushered. Then he'd take Murphy by the elbow and say: "That place has changed. That place ain't the same. That place ain't the levee. Stick with me and I'll show you the goddamned levee."

But it was no use. The upholsterer could not find or show Murphy the levee, the true and elusive levee that he alone could find and show. They were saved from their search by the upholsterer's wife. Though it had begun to set, the sun was still hot and each time he blinked Murphy thought he saw the upholsterer's wife. Like a squaw to a travois, she was hooked to the front bumper of the camper. She was rigged in a harness like Charles Atlas and was pulling the camper around and around the levee.

Around the nose and mouth, the upholsterer looked numb and very drunk. Swaying against a blue anemia of neon, he stood in front of the last tavern along the levee. When Murphy stopped beside him, the upholsterer put a hand on his shoulder and said: "OK, you won't let me show you the levee, you won't even let me show you how to handle a knife, but will you at least help me look for my wife?"

Looking over his shoulder, Murphy saw that the upholsterer had already found his wife. In the alley alongside the tavern, two campers were parked. One was new and the other was old. The old one bore faded decals of striking bass and pike, had a broken door that only bolted closed from the outside and a sign stenciled across the back bumper that read WARNING THIS VEHICLE STOPS AT ALL BARS. Flicking open his switchblade knife, the upholsterer went after the wrong camper, the new camper, the camper that looked like it ought to be owned by someone with a gun, someone who might come out of the tavern and blow the upholsterer's head off.

Head down, the upholsterer stumbled toward it as if he didn't want to be distracted from the mistake he was making, a mistake he seemed confident Murphy would correct. He went after a back tire very slowly and tentatively, as if he were waiting for Murphy to walk up and stop him. Squatting with his back to the old camper, the right camper, the upholsterer did not look like a wronged husband set on revenge, he looked instead like an aging pump jockey who had picked up the wrong tool, he looked like a red-headed fool trying to change a tire with a switchblade knife.

Walking over and squatting alongside him, listening to the tick and peck of his timid labor, Murphy knew he had to stop him. When he reached in a hand to do so, he wasn't quite surprised to come up with blood.

There wasn't much, but there was enough. Both Murphy and the upholsterer stood up. Looking from the camper tire, to his hand, to the switchblade knife, Murphy said to the upholsterer what he had said to him only a moment before: "You've got the wrong camper. You'd better put away that knife."

Even as he spoke the words, Murphy stumbled backward. It wasn't until the upholsterer put away the switchblade knife, it wasn't until he told Murphy to "Wait," that Murphy felt as if he had waited long enough; that if he waited even a second longer, he might wind up with his name and picture in the papers.

This thought made Murphy turn and run. He didn't stop until he'd put three billboards and a bowling alley between himself and the last tavern on the levee, until he'd found a service station restroom, washed his hand and wrapped it three times with toilet paper. Then he replaced his hurry with a firm decision.

Shut of the upholsterer's drunkenness, Murphy realized that he himself was far too drunk to continue home. If he did go home he would only cause trouble, only worry and hurt his mother and father. He had already done that, he told himself, often enough. Therefore, he would not go home. If the upholsterer could come to Decatur, if he could closely approach his father's house yet never enter it, so could Murphy. He was going, he told himself, to walk straight from that restroom to the corner of Prairie and Church. He was going to spend the night, by god, at the YMCA.

That night Murphy dreamed a dream about the levee. If it was the levee, why was there no water, no barges, no embankment, no Mighty Mississippi or even a slimy Sangamon nearby? *Because,* Murphy's mother said, *water seeks its own level. You can always tell a man,* Murphy's father said, *by the company he keeps.*

Throughout the night, the telephone kept ringing. The calls were from bartenders all along the levee. Though in his dream Murphy had not abandoned the upholsterer on the levee, though he had brought him along to the YMCA and had even taken off his shoes and tucked him into bed, the bartenders kept calling and telling Murphy if he didn't come down and get his buddy, his buddy was going to end up dead, somebody was going to relieve the son of a bitch of his goddamned head.

Each time the bartenders called, Murphy walked across the room to see if the upholsterer was still in bed. Each time he pulled back the sheet, he found the upholsterer dead asleep with his arms crossed across his chest.

After awhile, though, after it had rung thirty or thirty-five times, Murphy got tired of getting up to answer the phone, tired of walking the length of the room to see if the upholsterer was still in bed. In order at last to get some sleep himself, to silence the bartenders and the telephone, Murphy slipped into bed alongside the upholsterer. As soon as he pulled the sheet up over both their heads, as soon as he too crossed his arms across his chest, the levee broke and all the bars along it filled with water. Floating atop the flooded gutters and campers of the levee, borne along on water that could go ahead and seek whatever level it wanted to, Murphy sought and found a sleep at least as deep as the comatose upholsterer, the strange bedfellow who lay so still beside him.

When he awoke the next morning, Murphy knew two things and two things only: that he was in his parents' house and that it had never been locked. The camper door had never been locked. All the way to Decatur, except when they were actually banging and rattling along at eighty miles an hour, the camper door had never been locked. Murphy had wanted it to be locked, but it had not been locked. When he left the first tavern at which they stopped, he found the camper door halfway open. Though the blunt blond man had walked him outside, though he had even patted him on the shoulder, he hadn't locked the upholsterer in the camper at all. Sitting atop a roll of foam rubber, the upholsterer was nodding and drooling. But Murphy couldn't stop deluding himself. Standing at bar after bar, he continued to think of the upholsterer as *that poor son of a bitch locked out there in the camper*. Each time a cash register rang and sprang open, it seemed to charge Murphy's drinking with a loyalty high, light and hurried. Striding from bar after bar to unlock a camper that did not need to be unlocked, to spring an upholsterer who did not need to be sprung, Murphy himself felt sprung, drunk, crazy. Now he only felt indecent. Tightening his grip on a pillow he found clasped between his legs, thinking of the open camper door, the nodding and drooling upholsterer, a limerick popped into Murphy's head. It was about a maid from Decatur who'd gone to bed with an alligator. Murphy could not remember all of it, but he knew that after the alligator laid her, he ate her. Lying in bed in his parents' house in Decatur, Murphy knew that he had neither laid nor eaten the upholsterer, nor had the upholsterer laid or eaten him. Thinking back on yesterday, however, Murphy felt as if he might just as well have spent it smooching, necking and wrestling with a reptile; the counterfeits and condescensions, the manias and manipulations, the lies and lewd loyalties by which he'd brought himself once more to Decatur seemed now just that savage, perverse, putrescent.

Hungover and sick, his teeth hooked to the back of a hand he now realized the upholsterer had only creased across the palm with his switchblade knife, Murphy fervently wished his nose were made of metal. If so, it might have rusted overnight to the cotton of his pillow. But it wasn't rust that held his nose to his pillow, it was blood and Murphy knew how it had gotten there. It had gotten there because Murphy hadn't gone to the YMCA at all; he had gone to The Office instead. A pig knuckle, shuffleboard, St. Louis Cardinal bar, The Office wasn't far from Murphy's parents' house. Above the cash register there was a color photograph of Red Schoendienst in a St. Louis Cardinal baseball uniform. Each time the cash register rang and sprang open, it seemed to brighten the smile on Red Schoendienst's face until, Murphy's elbow slipping again and again off the bar, the bartender shut him off and offered him a cup of coffee. When Murphy said that he didn't want any coffee, the bartender offered to call him a cab. Even before he told the bartender that he'd taken enough cabs that day, Murphy seemed to be stumbling up a hill called IP&L hill.

Steep and barren, it rose above the tracks of the Illinois Central. Vaguely Murphy was aware of the lights of Decatur, that from where he staggered and stumbled he could see the smokestacks of the soybean-processing plants, that that tin can, bill-board, power pole hill was a place appropriate to his plight and mood. Though the bartender hadn't thrown him out of The Office, though he hadn't even asked him to leave, over and over Murphy muttered to himself: "They threw me out, they threw me out, the sons a bitches, by god, threw me out." Each time he spoke them, the words seemed to gather force and come at Murphy from behind, as if when he left The Office quietly and of his own accord someone had snuck up and shoved him from behind and it was the force of that shove that finally felled him, that made the ground, just at the crest of IP&L hill, rush up so fast to slam him in the nose.

It was like a baseball bat, Murphy thought, but there were cinders in it too. The hill was owned by the power company and a little farther down its slope, a hand hooked into a Cyclone fence that read DANGER HIGH VOLTAGE, Murphy vomited with a force that seemed cyclonic. Though he knew it wasn't, Murphy remembered his vomit as being blue and barometric, the rum in it laced with a kind of lightning that made him want not only to lie, but to roar out his lie.

It was a stupid lie and Murphy told it to his father. With bloodied nose and vomit-spotted shoes, Murphy stumbled up the front steps of his parents' house and waving his toilet paper—wrapped hand in front of him, had said to his father: "Did you ever have a guy pull a knife on you? Did you ever have to put somebody out with a single punch, with a single right hook to the head?"

Murphy tried not to remember what else he'd said, but he could not forget the pride he'd felt to have had someone "pull a knife on him," the hurry with which he'd stumbled home to wave his toilet paper-wrapped hand in front of his father's face. Recalling the slowness and difficulty with which his father had unlocked the screen door and let him in, Murphy lifted his head off his blotted and rusted pillow, pulled on his trousers, stumbled across the living room into the bathroom and locked the door.

Swaying above the bowl, Murphy pissed with a force that forced his hand into his back pocket. From it he withdrew the card he knew he'd find there. It was green and it said:

> EXCUSE ME I AM A DEAF MUTE
> I am selling this card with the sign
> language to enable you to understand
> some of the problems confronting the
> DEAF MUTE. Will you kindly buy one?
> Pay any price you wish.

Evidently, the price Murphy had paid was fifteen dollars. Because on the back of the card he found, as he knew he would, the upholsterer's signature. Tilden Joe Jolley, followed by "I.O.U. $15."

Vaguely Murphy could remember a sidewalk on the levee, the flickering hands of the man from whom, for a quarter, he'd bought the card in the first place. But a bit too quickly and dizzily, that transaction lost itself in the slurred letters and numbers of the upholsterer's I.O.U. Aiming and splattering very squarely in the toilet bowl, it seemed to Murphy that all afternoon long the upholsterer had been trying to sell him something. That something, Murphy decided as he flushed the toilet, was a seat next to his own in a paddy wagon.

As if to reinforce that notion, Murphy's father knocked on the bathroom door. When Murphy unlocked and opened it, his father handed him the Sunday *Decatur Herald and Review.* Pointing to an item on page two, he asked Murphy if that was the man he had been telling him about, the one who had cut him with a switchblade knife.

It was the upholsterer all right. Tilden Joe Jolley, age forty-two, had been arrested for drunk and disorderly conduct, for resisting arrest and for carrying a dangerous weapon. Bail had been set at $500.

Murphy, however, denied it. Shaking his head, he handed the newspaper back to his father and said: "No, Dad. I don't think that's the guy."

But his father seemed not to have heard or believed him. Turning away and taking off his glasses, he cautioned Murphy once more about the company he kept: "Keep running around with that kind of company, son," he said, "and you're going to wind up with your name and picture in the papers."

Not fifteen minutes after his father warned him about the company he kept, having begged off breakfast, having decided instead to take a little walk, to look for a duffel bag he had lost and knew damned well he would not find, Murphy saw someone he hadn't seen in years. Murphy saw Abraham Lincoln. Or rather he saw a perennial Decatur crazy who thought that he was Abraham Lincoln.

Still shaking his head, still caught somehow in the act of lying to his father, of handing the newspaper back and saying: "No, Dad, I don't think that's the guy," Murphy was walking along, thinking about the upholsterer. The poor son of a bitch who yesterday had never, not once, been *locked out there in the camper,* was now today in fact locked up in the county jail. What was Murphy going to do about it? In order to erase or pay for the lewd effusions of yesterday's drunk, to befriend someone who had never been and could never be his friend, Murphy thought he ought to face the upholsterer sober, ought to walk uptown and somehow go the upholsterer's bail for him. But when he thought to do so, when he thought of the bondsman he'd have to contact on Sunday afternoon, of how, if he were successful at so doing, he'd have to borrow the bondsman's fee from his father, Murphy did not mutter, but felt very much like muttering: "What I need is a goddamned lawyer."

It was precisely at that moment that he looked up and saw the man who thought that he was Abraham Lincoln. The timing was so stunning and hungover, the man so shocked, mocked and embodied his need for legal aid, Murphy wanted to run up and stop him, to engage him as a lawyer, to walk with him to the county courthouse where, in his shawl and his stovepipe hat, the man who thought that he was Abraham Lincoln would represent the upholsterer, would somehow post his bail, would somehow get the upholsterer out of jail.

But Murphy neither ran up to nor stopped the man who thought that he was Abraham Lincoln. Instead, he suffered a sort of syllogism: if at the moment he most suspected that the upholsterer was locked up in the county jail, his father had knocked on the bathroom door to confirm his suspicion, it somehow followed that, at the moment he most needed a lawyer or legal aid, the man who thought that he was Abraham Lincoln should appear on the sidewalk in front of him. Given the drift of his weekend, Murphy thought, he could no more walk the Sunday morning streets of Decatur and *not* run into the man who thought that he was Abraham Lincoln, than the man who thought that he was Abraham Lincoln could keep from leading him, as he was leading Murphy now, to the defunct barbershop in front of which, some twenty-five years ago, a squat and powerfully built young Negro had punched his father square in the nose.

The handkerchief was large and white. Long before the man drew it from his pocket, long before he bent his face toward it, Murphy knew that the man who thought that he was Abraham Lincoln would stop just in front of the barbershop to blow his nose. But when Murphy caught himself hoping for hemorrhage, for the great white honking handkerchief to bloom with blood, he made himself a vow.

Turning away from the man who thought that he was Abraham Lincoln, walking away from a barbershop that had once housed precinct headquarters, Murphy promised himself *never again* to ask his mother about the Negro and the punch his father had taken in the nose in front of precinct headquarters. It had become, that memory, a brief of grievance so worn and irreducible, Murphy vowed never to reduce himself to it again.

Just before he left that afternoon, his father set a seal on that vow. Handing over a loan of forty dollars, looking Murphy straight in the eye, his father said: "Why do you come home just to hurt us? Do you know, son, that less than 3 percent of the people in this country are like you?"

The Roaring Margaret

Iᴛ is not a caution sign, but the sign gives me caution.

As cautiously as I can, I say: "Did you see that sign back there?"

Beth says: "What sign?"

"The one we just passed. The one put up by the U.S. Fish and Wildlife Commission."

"No," she says. "What did it say?"

Marking the turn-off for a trout hatchery, the sign said "The Roaring Margaret," but when I get ready to say it said "The Roaring Margaret," I hear a sort of roaring in my ears that says I'd better not say what the sign back there said.

So I say: "I don't know. I didn't get it all. Something about spawning, something about a trout hatchery."

Something in my voice turns Beth toward me. She is my second wife and from the look she gives me, I know she knows I'm leaving something out. That something is this. In leaving out the name of the trout hatchery we've just passed, I'm leaving out the name of the wife who, some seven years ago, I left.

Her name, too, is Margaret and when I think of her as "The Roaring Margaret," I think how often, in the last half hour, keeping it to myself, I've thought about her, my father and my son.

Also about a yellow jelly glass.

For the last half hour Beth and I have been onto a touchy subject. We have been talking about birth control; we have been talking about using a diaphragm. I am no longer averse to using a diaphragm, but I am still averse to talking about using a diaphragm, because behind my talk, regressing at the behest of a gasp from a bathroom, a call for help from Margaret, I see myself, age nineteen and newly married, standing in the kitchen of the one-room efficiency apartment in which I first lived with Margaret.

Facing a traffic signal sort of decision, choosing between red, green and yellow, I snap up a yellow jelly glass and head for the bathroom.

Kneeling before the toilet from which Margaret's just arisen, coaxing from the bowl placental material somehow made more red and gelatinous by the jelly glass in which I trap it, I seem to hear in the rip of the waxpaper, the snap of the rubber band with which I seal the yellow jelly glass, a question Margaret will ask in the taxi on the way to the doctor's office: *if I've had a miscarriage Michael,* she says, *are you going to tell your parents?*

A good question, one that sees us not only to the doctor's office, but sits me in his waiting room, it calls less for an answer, than an act of medical intervention.

If, intervening in my behalf, a doctor confirms the contents of the yellow jelly glass, if I'm somehow able to relay that information to my mother, if she in turn says to my father: *Michael said that Margaret said that the doctor said she'd had a miscarriage,* will those words convey what I myself, for a month and a half, have been unable to admit to either of my parents: that Margaret was pregnant when we got married?

A hard question made harder by a question I hope the doctor's receptionist won't ask: *do I want my jelly glass back,* it's made harder still by a question that, to the jolt and jounce of a second taxi, Margaret can't help but ask.

The Roaring Margaret

So anyway Michael, she says, *now that I've miscarried, what do you think about what the doctor said? What do you think about him fitting me for a diaphragm?*

Trying to think what I think about a doctor fitting Margaret for a diaphragm, trying not to think about the removal from our kitchen of the rest of a set of glasses, a smashing against the wall of a railroad underpass, first of a green, then of a red jelly glass, I'm not surprised that, very soon after the doctor fits her for it, Margaret's diaphragm proves itself to be a kind of trap.

Margaret's diaphragm is not a trap. But because she's new to the use of it, because she doesn't anticipate the volume of blood it will trap if it's in place at the beginning of her period, I hear from the bathroom of our apartment, a second gasp. Then I hear Margaret say: *I started my period with my diaphragm in. There's so much blood, Michael, it reminds me of the miscarriage.*

Me too. Even as I get out of bed, even as I say for a second time: *let's see,* I see what Margaret means: matching the blood of a month ago, the blood in the bowl so suggests another trip to the kitchen, I'm thinking again of a yellow jelly glass when, for a second time, someone intervenes in my behalf.

This time it's not a doctor, it's Margaret's mother. Even as Margaret flushes the toilet, the telephone rings on the first of three calls which, increasingly brief, ease me out of mania into misericord: Margaret and her mother don't need to talk, they need to visit. If, that is, a visit's all right by me.

Walking Margaret to the bus station, seeing her off on a Greyhound that will take her 125 miles north to her parents' home in a town on the Illinois River, I stop, midway back to our apartment, on a low bridge above a nameless creek.

An urban trickler turning through truck tires, burst boilers and gutted innersprings, the wobble of its water bespeaks a weak-kneed truth: if you are nineteen years old and averse to your wife using a diaphragm, if you are even more averse to hav-

ing your father discover that your wife is using a diaphragm,
then you will do, on the afternoon of the morning of that discov-
ery, something perverse with your wife's diaphragm.

I do. I throw it into a creek.

I do not do so at the bidding of my father. But when I hear
again the plop of rubber in water, I hear at the same time, a
knock on a door. Also, playing on my patronymic, an old, old
logic.

If a pullout bed is a Murphy bed, if it's even more so with a
Murphy in it, if my name is Michael Murphy and if, at a little
after eleven A.M. in midweek of Margaret's week-long visit to her
mother, my sleep seems deepened by the name of a bed in which
Margaret is no longer lying, then all it takes is a knock on the
door to get this day, a wan Wednesday, started.

That and a flutter of the family throat. When nervous, the
males in our family tend to choke. The feeling is feathery but
real, a sensation of shadow one could, with the right kind of
cough, cough up.

Both my father and I suffer from this affliction, and when,
after his third triple knock, I unlock and open the door, a mutual
muscle seems to spasm in our throats.

Coughing, then choking, heading immediately for the bathroom of our one-room efficiency apartment, my father says:
what's this your mother says about Margaret visiting her mother?

When I say: *she'll be back at the end of the week,* my father clicks
on the light, snaps shut the door. Then he speaks a thought he
hates to think.

I hate to think son, he says, *that you were still asleep. I hate to think I
just woke you up.*

I don't. Clad only in underwear, coughing in counterpoint to
my father's coughing, I hate to think of Margaret's diaphragm.

If I'm not mistaken, Margaret's diaphragm is on the back of
the toilet in front of which, dressed in his suit and tie and the

strictest, most dignified overcoat he owns, my father's now standing.

Pearl gray in its pearl gray compact, resting in protective powder, flanked by a tube of jelly that seals its seal on the uterine cervix, Margaret's diaphragm is a birth control device at which my father, a deeply devout Catholic, doesn't like to look.

But from the quiet of the bathroom, from the slowing of his coughing, I know that's what he's doing, looking at Margaret's diaphragm.

There's nothing dirty about Margaret's diaphragm. Nor is there anything very biblical about my father. Yet if he were to murmur: *unclean son of an unclean marriage to a woman made unclean by the rubber in the powder in the compact on the back of the toilet,* if he were to rage white-haired out of the bathroom to scream at me: *get thee gone to the waters of Babylon,* he couldn't send me any straighter up the street to drop a pearl gray diaphragm into a milk gray creek.

The creek is not called "The Roaring Margaret." Nor would the U.S. Fish and Wildlife Commission be inclined to establish on its banks any trout hatchery. But when, reified by the sign we passed about a half mile back, I hear again the roar Margaret roared when I told her what I'd done with her diaphragm, when that roar seems to incorporate about eleven months later, the cries of our infant son, when I find myself thinking: *I'd do it all over again for Michael,* I'm tempted to say to Beth what I've already said to her a couple of times too often: *I can't wait to pick up Michael.*

But I don't. Instead, I say: "I can't wait to go hiking."

"Neither can I," Beth says. "What time did you say we're going to pick up Michael?"

I am about to say: *between one and three in Colorado Springs on Sunday,* when those words are undercut by a curse.

"Damn Beth," I say, "what's this?"

"What's what?"

"This red light below the odometer."

"I don't know, what's it say?"

Leaning forward, I say: "It says 'Alternator Warning Light.'"

Popping open the glove box, riffling quickly through the pages of the owner's manual, Beth says: "How long's that been on?"

"I don't know. Five seconds, maybe longer. I just now noticed it."

"Christ Michael," she says. "It says here to stop, it says to cut the engine."

Even before I stop, I cut the engine. Throwing our new VW Bug into neutral, turning off the ignition, I coast to a gravel-crunching stop on the shoulder of the road. Then I take the owner's manual from Beth.

> It reads:
> Alternator Warning Light.
> Stop at once. . . . *Turn the engine off!* Check first whether the V-belt is slipping or broken. The V-belt not only drives the alternator, but also the fan that cools the engine. Replace or tighten the belt.

"The V-belt's OK," I call out to Beth. "It's tight as a drum."

"Then if the manual's right," she says, "it's probably the voltage regulator."

The manual's right. It *is* the voltage regulator. But it isn't the voltage regulator that begins to boil, bubble, reek. The battery does that.

Located below the back seat, held in place by flat black straps that suggest to me the straps of an electric chair, the battery looks, when I look at it, like it's straining at its straps.

Staring at its positive and negative posts, thinking that if the battery had a mind those posts would be driven Frankensteinian into its temples, I'm trying not to grind my teeth, when I hear Beth say: "Look at it froth. It's burning my eyes and it's hurting my throat."

"We'll keep the windows down."

"But there aren't any back windows *to* keep down."

"I know that Beth."

"It can't do anything, can it? I mean it can't explode or catch fire?"

Saying: "No Beth, I don't think a battery can explode and I doubt it can catch fire," I not only exhaust my false knowledge of automobile batteries, I hear, at the first service station we come to, an automotive term I've never heard before.

So does Beth. Lowering her voice, tapping the glass of the odometer where earlier the mechanic reached in to tap it, she says as he said: "Disregard the idiot light. Just keep the windows rolled down and don't strike any matches. All you need is a quick charge to get you as far as Grand Junction."

Though I like the lowering and roughing of Beth's voice, the tapping of her fingernail against a glass the mechanic himself tapped, her miming of the striking of a match she takes from a pack I hadn't realized was in the glove box, I am an idiot for whom, as I drive to Grand Junction, it is extremely difficult to disregard the idiot light.

Trying not to think what it would be like to roll up the windows and to start striking matches, to conduct a road test of the explosibility and flammability of the gases released by a boiling battery, I stare like an idiot at the Alternator Warning Light.

Certain it snapped on just as we passed a sign put up by the U.S. Fish and Wildlife Commission, I can't help but wonder what we'd seen and heard had we turned off at the turnoff for "The Roaring Margaret" trout hatchery.

Thinking vaguely of a hatchery built to hatch a trout called the yellow jelly, a glassy and abstract fish the even glassier eggs of which I know, if I worked there, I'd find extremely difficult to abstract, fertilize, incubate, I'm so aroar with the little red roar of the Alternator Warning Light, I don't see coming, just up the road in Grand Junction, what I ought to see coming.

That something is this: though there is a voltage regulator fully covered in our warranty, there isn't a single voltage regulator in all of western Colorado.

It is a fact that calls, I guess, for a backward sweep of the hand. Also for a smock, a shock of white hair, a clipboard, a cleft chin, a pair of horn-rimmed glasses. That and a background, just up the hill, of a fenced-in power station. Thinking vaguely of a regulatory commission, one that would regulate the flow of voltage regulators to all of western Colorado, that if there were such a commission and it needed a commissioner, he might make a good commissioner, I look again at the service manager of the authorized VW dealership in Grand Junction.

With another backward sweep of his hand, he tells me what he's told me a couple of times already.

There aren't many bugs in these new Bugs, but the voltage regulator is one. He doesn't know, he says, how many voltage regulators he's had to replace in the last couple of weeks, but he does know this: he's fresh out of voltage regulators and since it's Friday, it'll be late Monday, maybe early Tuesday before he can get more in.

Before he can say it again, I turn away. Doing so, I pat a map I carry in my right back pocket. A trail map of the national park to which I've promised to take my twelve-year-old son Michael, a map on which I've marked trails I can't wait to hike with Beth and Michael, it tells me I just can't stand here patting my back pocket, I've got to walk across a gravel parking lot in Grand Junction, Colorado, I've got to enter a telephone booth, I've got to dial a number I do not want to dial.

That number belongs, as it has for years, to Margaret's mother. Rehearsing its familiar digits, I seem to hear from Margaret's mother, a question that I've heard before: *so what's the trouble now?*

Though now the trouble's automotive, the deeper trouble seems to be with me, my idiotic certainty that a sign put up by the U.S. Fish and Wildlife Commission was meant solely as a curse on me.

Cursing the roar of "The Roaring Margaret," cursing too the little red roar of the Alternator Warning Light, I know I'm about to curse at Margaret's mother when, halfway to the telephone booth, Beth stops me.

"Look Michael," she says, "I don't much want to, but maybe I'd better be the one to talk to Margaret's mother."

Maybe Beth had better.

Punching into a telephone dial the prayer I know we do not have with Margaret's mother, praying anyway that Beth will somehow convince her to convince Margaret to wait two days in a motel in Colorado Springs for us to pick up Michael, I turn away from a triple stack of quarters, the slur of silver with which Beth so deftly pays for the call.

Tempted to fold my hands and go to my knees, to pray an arc around and around our car, a white, sulfuric-smelling VW Bug the thrown-open doors of which seem to have belched out a back seat that sits now on gravel, I'm only halfway across the parking lot, only halfway resigned to sit down and patiently await Margaret's mother's answer, when I hear the crunch of Beth's hiking boots behind me.

Thinking: *that was quick,* I turn and say: "Did you get her?"

"I got her all right."

"What'd she say?"

"She said no. She said absolutely not."

It's an answer that not only cancels our hiking trip with Michael, it packs us into the back of a VW mini van, it delivers us, with the white-smocked service manager at the wheel, to a motel just off the main junction of Grand Junction.

To enter room one of the Econo Motor Court is to reenter in a way the one-room efficiency apartment in which I first lived with Margaret. Also it's to arrive at a juncture in my life with Beth.

Because Beth wants to get off the pill to rid her system of the effects of the pill, because she wants to do so in order to ready herself, after six months of using a diaphragm, to have a baby, because I had so much trouble this morning talking about this, so much trouble speaking to Beth a simple *yes*, I walk to the window, I take a deep breath.

In a room with a ghostly floor plan, a room that features cooking privileges, a wealth of leftover paper plates and a full set of jelly glasses, a room equipped with everything but a pullout bed, everything but a Murphy bed, a room that might, if I let it, send me racing up the street to drop a pearl gray diaphragm into a milk gray creek, I hear Margaret say what she said when she finally stopped roaring: *you stupid shit, don't you know my diaphragm's none of your father's business?*

Though Margaret was, is and always will be right, I am thinking: *if I'd do it all over again for Michael, then I've got to do it all over again for Beth,* when I hear her butt a hip against the door.

"Open up Michael," she says, "I've got my hands full."

To relieve Beth of two very heavy sacksfull of groceries she's carried from a supermarket just across the road, is to welcome her to a sort of prison cell.

Though neither the door nor windows of room one of the Econo Motor Court are barred, though Beth's no dark-haired, darkly tanned wife come to cook her husband a monthly meal, come to pay him a conjugal visit, I cannot help but think so.

Telling myself that we don't have much time, that anytime now a triple knock will sound on the door, I make love to Beth in a bed I'd like to have pulled crashing down out of the wall.

Falling asleep, I awaken to find, on my way back from the bathroom, Beth's black bikini underpants bound in a tight elastic ball. Recalling how she stripped them down then kicked them over her head, the flash and length of her leg as it kicked upward, I pick them up and squeeze them. When I do, they seem valved and palpitant, less like a pair of panties than a heart, something I might put to my ear and hear the roar of a mountain stream in. But I don't put them to my ear, I untie them and lift them to my face.

Inhaling the closest of chloroforms, the deepest of ethers, I drift across the room to fall into a bed that, even as my head hits the pillow, sets me down on the road I drove this morning with Beth.

Leading down out of a high mountain pass, following the turns of a tightly twisting trout stream, the road comes as it must, to a sign put up by the U.S. Fish and Wildlife Commission.

Slowing to the roar of the Alternator Warning Light, turning off at the turn-off for "The Roaring Margaret" trout hatchery, I stop to pick up my white-smocked father.

Opening and closing the door, coughing a cough to which I cough in counterpoint, he adjusts the horn-rimmed glasses he isn't wearing. Then tapping a clipboard with nothing on it, he says: *it says here, son, that I'm the commissioner. So stop and strip. So cut the engine.*

Even before I stop, even before I cut the engine, I'm wearing nothing but my underwear and my father's dressed once more in the strictest, most dignified overcoat he owns.

Shifting into neutral, pulling into the gravel-crunching parking lot of "The Roaring Margaret" trout hatchery, I hear my father clear his throat. Then he taps the empty clipboard and says: *it says here to go inside. It says to see if her V-belt's slipping or broken.*

But Dad, I say, *Margaret and I aren't married anymore. We got divorced. We're both remarried.*

It says here to go inside. It says to take this with you.

To accept from my father the empty clipboard, to enter "The Roaring Margaret" trout hatchery wearing nothing but my underwear, to forget once and for all that Margaret and I ever got divorced, that we ever got re-married, is to perform the lowest and slowest of commissions.

Opening cabinet after cabinet, ripping waxpaper and snapping rubber bands, checking too the grave level of the yellow jelly glass, feeling in myself reserves of servitude that will keep me at this task forever, I'm about to slip into bed, about to see if her V-belt's slipping or broken, when I hear a voice whisper: *you crud, you bum, you yellow jelly.*

Margaret speaks but the word and a flywheel begins to turn, to belt out trout so quick, glassy and abstract, I completely forget, in the fury of my work, the acids and gases released by their hatching.

So does Beth. She is about to lean into the darkened door of "The Roaring Margaret" trout hatchery, about to strike a match, when I awaken to a shaking of my arm.

"My God Michael," Beth says. "You woke me up. You started screaming something about matches."

"Damn Beth," I say. "I dreamed I was back in bed with Margaret. I dreamed I was married again to Margaret. I dreamed the room was filling with gas and you were going to start striking matches."

"Well the room's not filling with gas and I'm not going to strike any matches. So just lie back. Just try to go to sleep."

I say: "Right Beth," but I don't. I get up and I check the stove. Turning the turned-off dials, I turn and say: "I just want you to know Beth that I *want* to have a baby."

"So do I Michael," she says. "But it'll be at least six months before we can do anything about that. So leave the stove alone. Come to bed. I'm tired and I want to get back to sleep."

I say: "OK Beth," but I don't. I stand here for a long time and I watch her.

Forty-Hour Devotion

T HERE is a bet we bet each time we approach her house and it goes like this: "I'll bet the first thing Mom says is: 'I'll bet you're just dead. Sit down, I've got supper ready, I'll bet you're just dead.'"

This is an old bet, a ritual, trip-ending bet, but now as we enter her kitchen and she says: "I'll bet you're just dead. Sit down, I've got supper ready, I'll bet you're just dead," her words and her kitchen, the smell of jumbo fried shrimp mixing with freshly baked tollhouse cookies, the martini makings I know I'll find in the pantry, the pop of my son opening a Coke and my own cracking open of an ice tray, predict a second bet. Tonight, unable to sleep, a hand hooked backhanded to my wife's hip, the articulation of her hip a handle by which I grip myself to her pregnancy and my happiness over it, I'll confess, I bet, something I've confessed before: lately when my mother greets us with her bet that we're dead, just dead, her words have a deadening effect on me.

So does gin.

Drinking my first martini, I submit to an old and benumbing metaphor. If all the roads, ramps and bridges I've driven today were laid out like a chain going glassier with each sip I sip, then the gin cracks the whip on our trip and it shatters. We are all sitting safely around a table laden with a sumptuous fried shrimp dinner and, ready already for a second martini, I have lost all track of what my mother and my wife and son are saying.

In front of me sits a large blue-and-yellow can of mixed nuts (no peanuts). First it's in front of my empty plate, nicely set off by the olives in my martini, then it's on my empty plate, becomes in a sense my dinner. My mother indulges me not only in this, but in a second and a third martini. She herself is drinking a beer and smoking a cigarette and in the lighting of the cigarette, in my own reaching across the table to light her Merit Menthol with a match I've taken from her hand, I register mild surprise. Without my ever having quite partaken of it, dinner is over, my son (I can tell by the much-diminished bowl) has put away a lot of tollhouse cookies and he and my wife are in the living room and the television set is on.

Lying on the thickly carpeted floor, Beth observes a discipline. Because the women in her family are inclined during pregnancy toward varicose veins, because she herself bears already along the backs of her knees a blue hint of what could become varicose veins, she has her legs elevated. Her legs are long and lovely, and it pleases me that, fighting a genetic inclination, she lies now on my mother's living room floor with her legs elevated.

Beth is my second wife, stepmother to the thirteen-year-old with whom she shares the living room and a part of my pleasure in the elevation of her legs comes I know at the expense of my first wife; had she been inclined during pregnancy toward varicose veins, she would have gotten them and gotten them good. Thinking of varicose veins as a vengeance, a blue bulging of the legs my first wife would have somehow wreaked upon me, I am stopped by a thought cautionary, Confucian: he who allows the misery of his first marriage to deepen his pleasure in his second is a fool who will get what he deserves.

What I get from my son is a cookie crumb–spewing request for more tollhouse cookies. In a voice hoarse with chocolate, still chewing the last of a stack he took with him to the living room, he says: "Hey Dad. You want to throw me those tollhouse cookies?"

Both his laziness and his language come from me. He knows of course that the tollhouse cookies are in a heavy cut-glass bowl that I can't possibly throw to him in the living room, that if I'm going to honor his request I'll have to get up and carry the tollhouse cookies to him in the living room, that, nailed to my chair with leftover road rattle and gin, that's the last thing I want to do. So, having myself eaten nine olives, a full economy-sized can of very expensive mixed nuts without a single peanut in it, having drunk all but the dregs of this my third martini, aware of the hypocrisy of what I'm about to say, I say: "Michael, don't you think you've had enough tollhouse cookies?" and my words plunge the house into a momentary silence.

Within it, The Incredible Hulk growls and my mother stirs. I say: "Mom, don't get up" and from the living room Michael says: "Grandma, don't get up," but when neither of us gets up, she does.

Her trip into the living room with tollhouse cookies is a quintessential one. Within it, I see a thousand such trips. As long as she's up, Beth too partakes of tollhouse cookies and it would not surprise me if, on her way back to the kitchen, my mother would reach over and feed a couple of tollhouse cookies to the creature turning huge and green and splitting the seams of his clothes on the TV screen. But she doesn't do that. Instead, sitting down again at the kitchen table, she gets very, very quickly to the subject of my first wife, the 2,000-mile move she's about to make to Missoula, Montana.

By the time I've dismissed my mood of removal, a sense of listening to my mother's words from somewhere west of the Mississippi River, the far edge of the 250-mile drive I've driven today to and from eastern Iowa to bring Michael to her house in central Illinois, my mother is talking about a travel agent, telling me that she checked the airfare between Decatur, Illinois, and Missoula, Montana, with a travel agent and from the way she keeps saying "prohibitively expensive," I can tell she wants me to ask how much, so I say: "How much, Mom," and she says: "Michael, you won't believe this."

"Yes I will."

"One-way or round-trip?"

"Round-trip."

"Four hundred and fifty dollars."

In my mother's spelling out of $450, I hear her old habit of murmuring the numbers as she writes out a check, how she'd murmur, for instance, "four hundred and fifty dollars and zero one hundred cents" as she wrote out a check for Michael's round-trip airfare from Missoula, Montana, to Decatur, Illinois, and, reading my mind, she says: "I'm afraid I just don't have that kind of money, Michael. I just don't think I can help with that kind of airfare."

Tempted to ask her who asked her to help with any airfare, I say instead: "Of course you can't, Mom," and, reaching across the table for the match she's detached from the pack, I light her Merit Menthol and count the *m*'s.

There are fifteen of them. My first wife's name is Margaret and having married a millionaire named Mason Manning Mundy the III, having had by him twin daughters named Megan and Mandy, she's moving in a little less than a month now to a mountaintop mansion just outside Missoula, Montana. Of course she's taking Michael with her and if you add to that the quadruple *m*'s of "Mason and all his miserable mucking money," a phrase I can't after three martinis seem to get off of, you come up with about nineteen *m*'s and tonight, lighting my mother's Merit Menthols, I mutter so many *m*'s they call after awhile for a final martini.

Since it's my fourth, I go heavy on the ice, a little light on the gin and in so doing seem to earn a change of states. When I sit down again at the kitchen table, I get from my mother a question not about Montana, but Wisconsin.

My mother says: "So Margaret and Mason and the twins drove

up to the farmhouse in Wisconsin," and even as I nod and say: "Michael said they took off real early this morning for the farmhouse in Wisconsin," the telephone rings and Beth calls out from the living room: "Michael it's Mason, he's calling from the farmhouse in Wisconsin."

Why this doesn't surprise me more than it does, I do not know. But walking into the living room, wondering if I shouldn't turn around right now, descend the stairs and take this call on the telephone in the basement, I fight a disquieting impression. With her feet propped up on the sofa, with the receiver extended in her right hand upward and toward me, with her eyes looking just a little wide, my wife seems to have been floored by the telephone she's answered.

Taking it from her, I notice that the phone book, open to the Yellow Pages, lies beside her. Wondering what she's been letting her fingers do the walking for, recalling vaguely some dinner conversation between her and my mother about a good used crib, I put the telephone to my ear and as if he can hear me doing so, Mason says: "Michael? Mason here. I'm calling from the farmhouse in Wisconsin."

I say: "Right Mason" and he says: "Look Michael I'm afraid we've got a little trouble up here."

"Oh?"

"Yeah. I think it involves Michael."

Turning me toward my son, Mason's use of our mutual name pulls my hand toward the TV. When I turn the volume all the way down, Michael says: "*Dad* we're watching The Hulk," but it isn't true.

Both he and Beth are watching me, not The Incredible Hulk and, stupidly, I enjoy the attention.

Particularly Michael's. Though he turned thirteen only four months ago, it seems like a year or two since I last really got his attention and, having gotten it, I want to keep it for awhile.

Keeping my answers short and neutral, saying "Yes Mason"

and "No Mason" and "Do you want me to call you back when we get things settled on this end of the line Mason," I keep Michael on the hook: as long as I don't say that this phone call is about him, he will, I know, assume it's about him and that assumption makes him do something strange. He removes, very slowly, the hat from his head. As he does so, Mason, as if he's explaining to me the very gesture Michael's just performed, says: "I don't think, Michael, we would have called you about this if it weren't for the business of the hat."

I say: "I was just thinking about that" and when he says: "I thought you might be," I try to do what I've just lied about, I try to think about Michael's hat.

If, as Mason and Margaret still allege, Michael stole from them thirty dollars in cash to buy his hat—a leather hat, a flop hat, a hat the shape and batter of which suggest to me a Huck Finn code of honor, one that would preclude transporting stolen money across the Mississippi River, especially in your old man's car—then maybe Michael has done just that.

Mason thinks so. Listening to him explain for a second time about a wallet into which last night in Iowa he placed $625 but which, when he arrived in Wisconsin early this afternoon, contained only $500, I can't stop thinking about the Mississippi River. Feeling the expansion bridge hum of my own crossing back and forth of it in a single day, I wonder again whether my thirteen-year-old son would be capable of transporting stolen money across the Mississippi River. Given the three martinis I drank for dinner, given the fact that, just having started another, I can't quite remember whether Michael took off his hat during dinner, Mason's missing money seems a matter I'd better immediately look into.

Saying: "OK Mason, I'll get back to you right away," I put down the telephone and say: "Michael that was Mason. He was calling from the farmhouse in Wisconsin."

"Dad," he says, "I *know* that was Mason, I *know* he and Mom are at the farmhouse in Wisconsin. What did he want?"

"For me to talk to you."

"What about?"

"Money matters."

"*What* money matters?"

"Come on Michael," I say, "we're going to the basement."

"To the *basement?*"

"That's right, to the basement."

To get to the basement we must pass not only through the kitchen (where, having left off the elevating of her legs in the living room, Beth has joined my cigarette-smoking mother at the table), we must also make a descent into family history. For twenty-five years, working six days and nights a week, from January first to March fifteenth, my mother made out income tax returns. She did this in her knotty pine–paneled basement office.

Marching Michael down the stairs, I'm hit with a ghostly din of adding machine and typewriter, a scent of ink eraser, carbon paper and desktop blotters advertising funeral parlors. Taking it in, I think again of the telephone in the basement. Blunt, heavy and black, smelling as it does of nicotine and income tax, it looks, with its old-fashioned knotted-up cord, custom-made for the matter at hand. Knowing exactly how the receiver will fit in my fist, I know I can do what I've said that I'll do: confront my son with the fact of the missing money, ask him if he took $125 from his stepfather last night or very early this morning in Iowa, call them back in Wisconsin and tell them what he said.

What he says is beautiful. Having preceded me hat in hand down the basement stairs, having listened to me repeat the words his stepfather has just spoken, Michael, shaking his hat above his head, says: "Beautiful, Dad. That's just *beautiful.*"

Under the harsh light of a naked bulb, Michael is right now

anything but beautiful. He's been lifting weights and, according to Mason and his mother, smoking a lot of marijuana. I have lifted very few weights, smoked even less marijuana. There is, however, about my son a new pumped-up pectoral tenseness that suggests to me that he's not only been doing a lot of bench presses, but sucking down and holding in his lungs a lot of fiery marijuana.

Also watching television. Like the figure growling and fuming now on the silent screen above our heads, Michael bends over and, tensing his already tense and pumped-up pectoral muscles, seems about to turn huge and green and burst the seams of his shirt and trousers with righteous indignation.

Instead, his voice still hoarse with tollhouse chocolate, he begins to curse a kind of credo. He cannot believe, he tells me, that Mason and his mother think he took their goddamned money, he cannot believe I think he took their goddamned money, he cannot believe I actually told them I was going to goddamned call them back.

I can. So can the basement. In chairs all around us, I feel the ghosts of taxpayers past. Solemn citizens in a solemn time of year, figures with rubber bands bound around their fists, with fans of envelopes and affidavits held tight to their chests, they present a silent consensus: any boy who can shout and shake his hat and fist and curse like Michael can, could not only steal $125 from his stepfather's wallet, he could transport, in his father's car, that money across the Mississippi River.

I don't want to believe it. Nor do I want, even for a minute, to confuse Michael's anger with his innocence. Therefore, to make absolutely sure I'm not afraid of making absolutely sure he didn't take the money from Mason and carry it in my car across the Mississippi River, I say: "Hold it a minute now Michael. Are you absolutely sure you didn't take that money from Mason?"

"Sure I'm sure."

"You don't know anything about it?"

"I don't know anything about it. I'm telling you, Dad, I didn't take Mason's money."

"OK. That's all I wanted to hear you say. I believe you. I'm calling Mason."

I can't get Mason. Even on my mother's blunt black basement telephone, I can't get through to the farmhouse in Wisconsin. Each time I try, I get a busy signal. Smiling at my party-line luck, chuckling over the *fuck* Michael mutters each time I shake my head and put the telephone down, the ghosts of taxpayers past laugh out loud when Michael finally says: "Look, Dad, that line might stay busy all night. If it's all right with you, can I try to catch the end of 'The Hulk'?"

I say "sure" and he says "thanks."

When, through the basement ceiling, I hear Michael turn the TV up, I picture a bluff above a river. Lifting over his head and hurling into the water a car like the car I drove twice today across the Mississippi River, The Incredible Hulk bends and growls a growl that, shaking a farmhouse in Wisconsin, makes a funeral parlor blotter hop on my mother's income tax table.

Having brought my fist down on my mother's income tax table just a little harder than I wanted, I hear Beth call from the kitchen: "Michael, are you all right down there?"

"Sure," I say. "Why don't you and Mom come on down? I need to talk to you."

Together, they descend the basement stairs. Along with her matches and Merit Menthols, my mother brings a beer and the watery remnants of my fourth martini. Pulling up two green plastic lawn chairs, Beth settles in one, elevates her legs on another. Sitting down in the chair she sat in for so many years, a chair positioned midway between the typewriter and the adding machine, my mother, squaring up her funeral parlor blotter, looks ready to come out of retirement, ready to get back to work on income tax.

Knocking back my martini and recounting Mason's phone call

from the farmhouse in Wisconsin, I try not to let my sense of Michael's innocence get mixed up with gin, Huck Finn and my own double crossing in a single day of the Mississippi River. "I've talked to him," I say, "I've confronted him and I really don't think he did it, I really don't think Michael took Mason's money."

Neither does my mother. But I'm not so sure about Beth. Sitting in my mother's basement with her legs elevated, she looks like a girl who's wandered in to have her income tax figured. Imagining some obscure exemption attached to her marriage to me, a tax benefit my mother alone would know how to figure, I am thinking of a refund the exact sum of Michael's round-trip airfare from Missoula, Montana, to Decatur, Illinois, when my mother says: "Well I don't like this, Michael, not one bit. And if worse comes to worse, if Mason and Margaret really do move to Montana and take Michael with them, I guess I'm just going to have to help with his airfare to and from Decatur."

"Come on, Mom," I say. "You know we can't ask you to do that. You know you don't have that kind of money."

"We'll see, Michael," she says, "we'll see."

When my mother says this, I see her as I used to see her, sitting at this very table, counting of a Saturday night, her income tax money.

Her fingers flying silver and numerical across the keys of the adding machine, the smoke of her cigarette rising blue to the ceiling, her hair done up in a mint green scarf with light green dimes and dollar signs showing in its folds, she'd recite our expenses and savings in a voice that seemed not only to catch and repeat the exhaustion and satisfaction of each and every taxpayer whom that week she'd served, but that says tonight, some twenty years later, if I just keep trying, if I just keep dialing the right number, I'll get, on my mother's blunt black basement telephone, Mason at the farmhouse in Wisconsin.

Forty-Hour Devotion

A pillow prayer isn't much of a prayer.

From a priest at a retreat I first heard that notion set forth: if you really mean it, he said, if you really want the Lord to listen, get out of bed, kneel on the floor, pray your prayer there.

Often I meant it, often I did as the priest told me I must do, I got out of bed, knelt on the hardwood floor, prayed my prayer there.

Now, though, welshing and waffling on an apostasy I find hard to practice at night, harder to practice in my mother's house, telling myself her carpets are so thick it wouldn't make any difference anyway, I allow myself to pray in bed, to emit snippets and spits of the Hail Mary or hacked Latin which, short-circuiting my brain and shaming the historical fact of my break with the church, use that shame to induce sleep.

So it was last night. To a *Deus Absconditus* of drivel, drool, pillow prayer, I prayed: *Dear Jesus let me get Mason at the farmhouse in Wisconsin, dear Jesus don't let that line stay busy all weekend long.*

Waking with those words still stuck in my mouth, telling myself that if I meant them last night I'll get immediately out of bed and onto the telephone this morning, I pull on a pair of Levis, pass through the kitchen with a greeting to Beth and my mother, and, coming fully awake neither to the beat of my bare feet on the basement stairs, nor the *butt, butt, butt* of the busy signal I get again from the farmhouse in Wisconsin, I hear my mother call from the kitchen: "Michael do you want coffee?"

"Yes."

"Do you want it down there?"

"Sure I guess."

In the cup-and-saucer clink of her descent of the stairs, in the thump of plumbing that says Beth has repaired to the bathroom above, I hear a murmur of *m*'s and, again and again, the mutual Michael that last night drew my hand to the TV set. Remembering that gesture, the way I turned the sound down on a green-turning creature to whom, only moments before, I'd imagined

97

my mother feeding tollhouse cookies, I seem to turn the sound down on everything but: "I kissed him goodnight, I blew out his votive light."

"You did what, Mom?"

"I kissed Michael goodnight, I blew out his votive light."

Thinking: *I thought I asked you not to do that, I thought you promised not to do that,* I inhale coffee steam and put together what I've missed: last night in a nightgown with a scapular safety-pinned to its shoulder strap and a pocket weighted with a vial of holy water she promised not to sprinkle on Michael, with one hand wrapped in rosary beads I've asked her not to pray in the presence of Michael, the air still sweet with the smoke of a blown-out votive light I know she agreed at least three years ago never again to light for Michael, my mother kissed my son goodnight and I am thinking: *what the hell, what the hell,* when I hear her say: "And then the poor thing. I felt so sorry for him. Do you know what he said?"

"What did he say?"

"He squeezed my hand and said: 'Grandma, you don't think I took Mason's money do you?'"

"What did you say?"

"I said: 'No Michael, I don't think you took Mason's money.'"

Neither do I. But again, I'm not so sure about Beth. Double-clutching, the bathroom above sends out a second shudder of plumbing that sounds skeptical, unsure: if he didn't take Mason's money, why would Michael sugar his grandmother with a question that in turn suckers me: "What about me Mom," I say. "Did Michael say anything about me?"

"What do you mean Michael?"

"I mean did he ask you if you thought I thought he took Mason's money?"

"No, he didn't."

"What about Beth? Did he ask you if you thought *Beth* thought he took Mason's money?"

"No, he didn't. But I'll tell you one thing, Michael. It's times like this I thank God I've got the Church, I thank God I've got my faith. Sometimes it's all that keeps me going."

Me too. Thinking of my faith in my mother's faith as a faith in bad taste, in blue votive lights, rhinestone rosary beads and cut-glass vials of holy water, I experience, for the first time this morning, true gin hangover: if my faith in my mother's faith is all that sometimes keeps me going, if Michael really *is* going with Mason and his mother to live in a mountaintop mansion just outside Missoula, Montana, then why *wouldn't* he steal $125 from Mason and transport it in my car across the Mississippi River?

As if he can hear the question I've just put to myself, Michael screams down from the front bedroom: "Dad, did you get Mason yet?"

"No, Michael," I yell back, "but I'm still trying."

Try I do. To the buzz and bump of a busy signal, to the juniper berry jump of a gin hangover, to the blue verboten of a blown-out votive light, I replay Michael's goodnight question, my mother's answer to it. Because she could not have said: *No Michael I don't think you took Mason's money* without giving Michael a good hard squeeze around the neck, I can't wait to get my hands around Michael's neck.

Not to wring it, but to rub it. Not to choke Michael into some wretched confession, but to touch him. It is with us a Saturday morning ritual, the rubdown. Always it takes place in the front bedroom and always it begins with the placing of my hands around Michael's neck. A shrugger of my hands from his neck and shoulders, a shunner of the hugs I try to give him, Michael has for the last three years or so, eschewed all attempts at physical affection. But he still lets me rub his back.

And afterward we always wrestle. To wrestle with Michael is to wrestle with a tag team coming at me out of the past. Dressed in Dr. Dentons and in dinosaur-print pajamas, inching up the support pole in the basement where we confirm in pencil that he's

growing like a weed, clad in weed-stained white Levis from playing kickball in a vacant lot after dark, going through orthodon-
tics made more menacing by the presence in his mouth not only
of braces but of rubber bands, wearing cut-off sweatpants that
resemble the riven trousers of the monster into which he seemed
last night to metamorphose, this tag team, taking on muscle and
made up of every Michael I've ever wrestled, getting old arm-
locks on my head, old hammerlocks on my arms, will ask as always the same question: *Give up Dad, give up?*

Nope.

A hope as well as an answer, that *nope* lifts me from my chair.
Standing barefooted and barechested before my mother's income tax table, screaming in my mind a *nope* so strident it shakes
a farmhouse in Wisconsin, I cannot wait to wrestle Michael.

First, though, I have to issue to my mother, the warning I
ached, on her blunt black basement telephone, to issue this
morning to Mason at the farmhouse in Wisconsin.

Leaning over, I say: "Well I'll tell you one thing Mom. I know
Michael and if they keep accusing him of taking their money,
he's going to *start* taking their money, he's going to *start* taking
every dime he can get."

Because I feel pride in my prediction, some inane inflating of
my paternal breast that makes me rap a knuckle against her income tax table, because my mother frowns and warns me not to
talk that way to Michael, not to go putting any ideas into Michael's head, I'm not surprised to find that, once I've gotten up
the basement stairs, across the living room and am sitting on the
side of his bed, the idea's already worked its way into Michael's
head.

As if I've rubbed the words into his back, as if they've moved
on their own up his spine, through his head and into the drool
he's drooling onto his pillow, I hear Michael mutter: "I hope you
know, Dad, that this isn't the first time Mom and Mason have
accused me of taking their money."

"I know it isn't Michael."

"It isn't even the *second* time they've accused me of taking their money. It's about the *third* or *fourth* time they've accused me of taking their fucking money."

"Watch the language Michael."

"Well, I'll tell you one thing," he says. "If they keep accusing me of taking their money, I'm going to *start* taking their money."

"Come on Michael," I say, "you're smarter than that."

"No I'm not."

Thinking: *neither am I, neither am I,* I start a tickle that starts a wrestle for which both of us are more than ready.

Imagining my hangover as a hangover of hardening glass, a crystallized mix of gin and holy water, I want to shatter and I want Michael to help me shatter, that hangover.

He does. Muttering: "No grabbing fingers Dad, no bending fingers Dad, no scratching Dad, no biting Dad, no twisting noses Dad," Michael, wrestling like all the Michaels I've ever wrestled, grabs and bends my fingers, scratches me, bites me, twists my nose.

Going for an armlock on my head, trying to get me full-nelson facedown on the pillow, dropping me with a thump to the floor, he gets a hammerlock on my arm. Kneeling in an attitude of enforced prayer, trying to imagine a prayer my son might wrench from me from behind, coming up instead with singsong Swedish incessance, the Hansen-to-Swenson-to-Jenson-to-Johnson dairy farmer gossip I keep imagining is keeping me from getting through to the farmhouse in Wisconsin, I feel, with my face grinding into my mother's carpet, a whole lot better.

In the cough and *oof* of my breath against mohair, I blow out gin. All of my nose, ear, chin, elbow, wrist and knee burns burn gin. Fighting dry heaves, I say: "Let me go Michael. You're breaking my arm."

"Too bad, Dad, too bad."

"Come on, Michael. Let me up."

"Give up, Dad, give up?"

A *nope* I'd have rattle the windows of a farmhouse in Wisconsin, my *nope* goes out only, it seems, to my mother.

Up the basement stairs, through the kitchen and across the living room, she comes. Arriving at the bedroom door, she says: "Now you two stop that wrestling. You're going to hurt each other. Do you hear me, do you hear me?"

Though we both hear her quite clearly, neither of us chooses to answer.

When we do not, my mother does something Irish, atavistic. She falls to her knees. I do not know how many grandmothers have in our family fallen to their knees beside sons and grandsons locked in hammerlock. I know only that my mother seems practiced at it. Like a stringy, septuagenarian wrestling referee, she slaps her hand three times on the carpet, whispers: "Now you two stop it," and Michael lets go of my arm.

Kneeling on the bedroom floor with Michael and my mother, trying not to think: *the family that prays together stays together,* I rise and head once more for the telephone in the basement.

Something there is in me that wants to declare an emergency, to get on the telephone in the basement and to call an operator and to lie, to tell an operator that there's an emergency and she's going to have to break in on the rural party line, the Swedish incessance, the Hansen-to-Swenson-to-Jenson-to-Johnson dairy farmer gossip I keep assuming is keeping me from getting through to the farmhouse in Wisconsin. But Illinois law forbids it. Also the ghosts of taxpayers past.

Seated according to the severity of the injuries they've survived by breaking in on rural party lines to get help for wives who've had coal-oil stoves blow up in their faces, for husbands who've gotten their right arms caught up to the elbow in augers, the ghosts of taxpayers past, having survived many farm mishaps, have, I know, their counterparts up in Wisconsin.

Thinking of men and women named Hansen, Swenson, Jenson, and Johnson who've survived coal-oil stove explosions and auger mutilations by breaking in on rural party lines up in Wisconsin, I tell Michael what I've been thinking all along: that it would not only be plain wrong to call an operator, tell a lie and declare an emergency, it would be downright risky.

"Risky," he screams. "What the hell do you mean *risky?*"

It's difficult to say exactly what I mean by "risky." But tempted to risk parable on Michael, to cite to him the story of the little boy who cried wolf, knowing that he wouldn't let me get very far with that, that he'd whisper: *screw the story of the little boy who cried wolf, Dad, what are you trying to say,* I say: "What I'm trying to say is this: screw around lying about an emergency, Michael, and you just might wind up bringing an emergency on."

That truth not only brings grave nods of the head from the ghosts of taxpayers past, it draws from Michael more prime-time pantomime.

Bending as if he's trying to lift off the floor and over his head the snarling iron emergency he might, by lying to a long-distance operator, bring down on his head, he gets into his face and into his pumped up neck, pectoral and arm muscles, a look so self-righteous and overinflated, I try to do what I know I shouldn't try to do. I try to touch him.

Snapping my hand backhanded off his shoulder, Michael says: "Knock it off, Dad, I'm pissed."

"Who isn't?"

"You, Dad, you get off on this shit."

"No I don't."

"Yes you do. You love to march me down the basement stairs and read me Illinois law from the telephone book. You don't give a *damn* that Mason and Mom still think I took their money."

"I do too."

"Prove it."

"How?"

"Get in the car and drive me up to Wisconsin."

"Come on Michael, we've already been through that. It would take all weekend."

"Then get on the phone and call an operator."

"No."

"Why?"

"Because declaring an emergency would be a lie and it's against Illinois law and I don't want to break the law and I don't want to be a liar either."

"Ha."

"What do you mean 'ha'?"

"I mean ha ha ha and ho ho ho and oh I hope you know, Dad, what this is doing to my stomach."

An old hope, one he's hoped before, it seems to come accompanied this time with a lifting of his own hands-off policy. Pulling up his T-shirt and thumbing a stomach in which three different doctors, studying three different sets of X-rays, could find no sign at all of ulcer, Michael seems to invite me to step forward to touch his stomach where his stomach hurts.

A doubting Dad who'd like to try to do just that, to let his index finger indicate all by itself the spot it ought to touch, I'd like right now neither to tickle nor wrestle Michael, but to reach out and snuff with a fingertip a stomach pain which, as it enrages him, frightens and baffles me.

"Goddamn it, Dad," I hear Michael say, "what's bugging you? Why are you looking at me that way?"

"What's bothering me, Michael," I say, "is what's bothering you."

"What?"

"What's eating at me," I say, "is what's eating at you."

"Come on, Dad," he says, "can't you talk straight for a change?"

"This telephone," I say. "We've got to get away from it for a while. We've got to stop trying to get Mason at the farmhouse in Wisconsin. We've got to get out of this house."

We've also got to get, according to my mother, something to eat.

"Michael," she calls from upstairs, "did Michael say his stomach hurts? Well I don't doubt it, not a bit. It's after eleven in the morning and you two haven't eaten yet. Now get up here and get something on your stomachs. I'm starting the eggs right now."

Starting at the same time a Saturday afternoon shopping trip.

With soft-boiled eggs, buttered toast, honey-sweetened tea and ice green lime sherbet, my mother not only soothes Michael's upset stomach, she fuels a shopping trip which, taking all four of us out the front door, through a cut-rate liquor store, a KarmelKorn shop, a discount record store, a Fannie May's, a Walgreen's, three used-furniture stores and the catalog department at Sears, lands us as it must, at Harry Applebaum's Haberdashery.

According to a sign in the front window, Harry Applebaum's Haberdashery ("66th Year Serving the Decatur Area") specializes in hard-to-fit boys. Michael is not a hard-to-fit boy. But he is a hard-to-please boy. In this he has plenty of company from boys and girls.

Through Bell Bottoms, Straight Legs, Boot Cuts, Flares and Original Levis Blue Jeans, through waxen stacks of ceiling-high denim that make Harry Applebaum's look more like a supply depot than a haberdashery, an army of teenage boys and girls riffle, jostle, giggle and buy.

So does Michael. And when he gets home, he scalds, he soaks. Bleeding ink black to indigo blue, emitting clouds of dye like intertwined, brass-riveted denim octopi, three pairs of Levis, their front pockets turned inside out, float in my mother's bathtub.

Tempted to kneel and dip my hand, to confer with a slurred sign of the cross a kind of blessing on my mother's indulging of Michael, I think a thought I kept thinking throughout our shopping trip: nothing, not even Mason's missing money, could spoil my mother's spoiling of us, could keep her from spending on us, this sunny Saturday afternoon, an awful lot of money.

Especially on Michael.

Looking down at the ink black bowl of her bathtub, thinking vaguely of bathtub gin, some ancient alcoholic concoction denatured enough to make the drinking of it dangerous, I feel as I often feel in my mother's house: drunk before I've ever touched a drop.

It's fun, of course, to feel in my mother's house, drunk before I've ever touched a drop. But it's also a precondition. If I meet it with a first martini, I know I won't be able to stop until I've had far too many martinis.

Therefore, paying a personal penance for my mother's sin of denim, I tell myself that I'm not going to have another martini until I get Mason at the farmhouse in Wisconsin. And as if to congratulate that resolve, just as I flush the toilet and turn from the bathroom, the telephone rings.

It ought, of course, to be Mason calling from the farmhouse in Wisconsin. But all afternoon and evening long it isn't. It is, instead, one of the disabled.

I don't know why, but when she was working, my mother made out income tax returns for a lot of the disabled. Especially telephone operators. From all over central Illinois, diabetically blind or arthritically crippled or half-deaf telephone operators came to my mother to have their income tax returns made out.

Thin and wrenlike, with oxygen-sick lips, tiny voices and wire-bright heads of yellow, orange and light blue hair, they carried into our basement a bitter, almost sisterly loyalty to my mother.

Under the press of their questions about the alcoholic brothers, married sons and jobless husbands they had to support, my mother, touching the point of her pencil to the tip of her tongue, would get to work. Working out their rough copies with a pencil and eraser, she'd encourage and certify every deduction, loss, expense and exemption her disabled telephone operators had decided, after much deliberation, to claim.

Now, though she's three years retired from the income tax business, her disabled telephone operators, all of them long since phased out of the telephone system, can't seem to leave my mother alone.

Taking their calls on the telephone in the basement, referring to files she still keeps current, saying: *You don't owe on that, Flo,* or *You paid that in April, Mabel,* or *You go ahead and submit that claim, Jane,* my mother dispenses to her disabled telephone operators so much free advice, I begin to wonder if, late this sober and sleepless Saturday night, we couldn't ask *them* for a little help.

Thinking of an ancient telephone station out in Bearsdale, Boody or Blue Mound, I imagine one of my mother's disabled telephone operators placing for me a powerful long-distance phone call. Plunging a burnished brass jack into a jet black switchboard, cracking a sort of telephonic whip back up the Mississippi River, my mother's disabled telephone operator might knock, with a crackling electric shock, Mason Manning Mundy or maybe my ex-wife Margaret to the kitchen floor of the farmhouse in Wisconsin.

Because I can see a bit too clearly how Mason Manning Mundy or maybe my ex-wife Margaret might look laid out on a linoleum floor with a telephone in their hand and their legs elevated on a kitchen chair, because that view seems not only unfair to them but to Beth too, I turn in bed toward her.

Over her eyes, as if to keep out the aberration that's keeping me awake, she's placed a damp washcloth. Touching her shoulder, I whisper: "Beth are you asleep?"

"No Michael," she says, "but I *want* to be asleep."

"Listen Beth, I'll keep this quick, but can I ask you a question?"

"Go ahead."

"You don't think Michael took Mason's money, do you?"

"Not if you don't, I don't."

"What does that mean?"

"That means, Michael, that you were the one who took him downstairs. You were the one who confronted him. You were the one who saw the look in his eyes when you asked him if he took Mason's money."

"That's right, I did. And I'm telling you right now, Beth, I don't think Michael took that money."

"Then neither do I."

"Good."

"So goodnight, Michael. Just lie still and try to go to sleep."

I can't sleep. Each time I close my eyes and try, I experience afresh this morning's hangover: if my faith in my mother's faith is all that sometimes keeps me going, if he really *is* going with Mason and his mother to live in a mountaintop mansion just outside Missoula, Montana, then why last night wouldn't Michael have kept right on going, why, working his way up a sort of hierarchy of hypocrisy, wouldn't he have ended by asking his kneeling grandmother if she thought *God* thought he took Mason's money?

Because I can just hear Michael saying that, reaching out, grabbing his grandmother's hand and saying: *Grandma you don't think* God *thinks I took Mason's money do you,* I'm not surprised to find that, once I finally fall asleep, I dream a dream about my mother's bathtub.

Kneeling where Michael knelt to do his drubbing, plunging my hands into the ink black waters of my mother's indulging of my son, *glad* that my mother loves my son so lavishly and so blindly, I mutter to myself: *unless I put my hand into all six of these front pockets and find all six of these front pockets empty, I shall not believe.*

Then turning from the tub, I turn to my naked, flop-hatted son who says: *Bring here thy hands and feel my empty hands, Dad, and bring here thy fingers and run them inside the band of my hat and be not unbelieving but believing, for amen, amen I say unto you, Dad, blessed are they who have not fallen asleep and have not dreamed and yet have believed for theirs is the kingdom of the freedom from the telephone.*

Slamming the telephone down on a last natter of laughter from the ghosts of taxpayers past, I know I'm going to get, when it's just a little too late to get it, when I no longer want to get it, a phone call from Mason at the farmhouse in Wisconsin.

I do.

Having just finished a massive breakfast of bacon and eggs and navy beans topped off by pecan pie a la mode, we're all sitting around the kitchen table, our bags packed and lined up in the living room, when the telephone rings.

Rising and whispering: "I'll bet that's Mason, I'll bet he's calling from the farmhouse in Wisconsin," my mother moves swiftly to get it.

Snapping it up in mid-ring she says: "Oh good it's you Mason. Listen, you won't believe this, but you just caught them going out the front door."

Why my mother has to lie this way, I cannot say. But her lie turns me toward the front door. Leaking brilliant Sunday morning sunlight, it looks less like a door through which Mason could have just caught the three of us going, than it does the blown-open cargo hatch of a jetliner.

Flying high above a Mississippi River Valley of missing money, busy telephones and borrowed airfare, bound ultimately for distant and prohibitively expensive Missoula, Montana, it's a jet-liner from which I feel right now an impulse to hurl myself, or if I'm somehow the jumpmaster, to kick Michael, Beth and my seventy-three-year-old mother.

But it's too late. Even as I feel above our heads the pop of four pale parachutes that would waft us safely down onto Decatur, I hear my mother call from the living room: "Michael, it's Mason, he's calling from the farmhouse in Wisconsin."

Rising to her bidding, I listen to my mother pull on me a very old, very unintentional trick: telling Mason all about the busy signal we've gotten for almost exactly forty hours now from the farmhouse in Wisconsin, about how we thought about calling an operator and declaring an emergency, but then thought better of it, she says: "But here's Michael, Mason, he'll tell you all about it."

Taking the telephone from my mother, I take a sort of Fifth Amendment: to all of Mason's questions about the busy signal we've gotten for almost exactly forty hours now from the farmhouse in Wisconsin, I answer so minimally and noncommittally, I draw from him a question I guess I want to draw: "What's the matter Michael," he says. "Did I get you at a bad time? Can't you talk?"

Nodding and saying: "Right Mason, hold on a second I'll be right with you," I put the telephone down and head for the basement.

It takes me a long time to get there.

On my way to the basement, I recall Michael's first response to Mason's allegation.

Speaking the word *beautiful,* Michael spoke in a way the truth: money placed in a wallet in eastern Iowa, money that showed up missing in a farmhouse in southwestern Wisconsin, cracking a telephonic whip down the Mississippi River, knocked my pregnant wife to the floor in central Illinois.

No, my pregnant wife was *already* lying on my mother's living room floor, but remembering the way in which, wide-eyed and pregnant, Beth held the telephone up to me, remembering how floored she looked by the telephone she'd answered, I take up, in taking up the telephone in the basement, a sort of gauntlet.

Thinking of a negative credo that I myself might shout, one in which, working my way up from Beth to my mother through the angels and the saints, I wouldn't stop shouting until I got to God, until I screamed: *Goddamn it Mason, I don't even think* God *thinks Michael took your money,* I say: "Listen Mason, I've confronted Michael, and I really don't think he did it, I really don't think he took your money."

"Good, Michael, I'm glad to hear you say that."

"I'm glad, Mason, to be able to say it."

"But the only thing is, Michael, we've come up with something on this end of the line."

Clapping my hand over the phone and yelling: "Hey Michael, hey Mom. I've got it down here. You can hang up up there," I feel, to the click of a receiver coming down, dumbfoundedness tick through me.

Saying: "What's that you said again now Mason?" I hear Mason say: "I said, Michael, that we've come up with something on this end of the line."

"Oh. What's that?"

That's this. They have, do Mason and Margaret, a fellow who keeps a key to their house down in Iowa, a young bachelor named Ray, who, having been asked to do so this morning by Mason and Margaret, turned up, when he had a look around Michael's room, an empty Excedrin bottle he said smelled like grass and also some cash.

"How much cash, Mason?"

"Not much, Michael. Only about three bucks. But the thing is, when Ray was getting ready to lock back up, a kid came up on a bike looking for Michael."

Up the sidewalk, looking a little like Michael, I see the kid coming, a torn T-shirted, muscle-pumped kid on a high-seated, ten-speed Schwinn. When he triple-grips to a stop in front of Ray, I hear Mason say: "Well, Ray said the kid said Michael owed him fifty dollars."

"Fifty dollars?"

"That's right and Ray said the kid said Michael said he was going to get the money this weekend from his Grandma in Illinois."

When I say "Oh," Mason says: "So anyway Michael, we don't want to butt in but the thing is, we just don't think Michael should have that kind of money to spend. At least not right now. At least not to repay a debt he shouldn't have incurred in the first place."

"Right Mason. So what do think we should do?"

"I don't know."

Thinking: *Neither do I, neither do I,* I hear myself say: "OK, Mason, I'll tell you what. Michael's coming back to Iowa broke. I mean with his pockets absolutely empty. I mean with his pockets turned absolutely inside out. I'll take care of that much on this end of the line."

"OK, I'll deal with the rest when we get back down to Iowa. So long Michael."

"So long Mason."

Long, long do I sit at my mother's income tax table.

Oh, what a gas for the ghosts of taxpayers past. From lawn chairs and folding metal chairs, one by one, they rise and advance toward me. With rubber bands bound round their fists, providing fistfuls of sharp, sharp pencils, spreading out white affidavits before me, they whisper: *If you're pissed at Mason, sign this form, if you think that Mason with all his money couldn't touch your rich, rich weekend in Decatur, sign this form, if you want to claim the total exemption of the ink black martini, sign this form, if you could absolutely drown in drunken spite of Mason and your ex-wife Margaret, sign this form.*

Shaking my head and pushing back their forms, I call out: "Hey Mom. Can I talk to you for a second? Down here please?"

Ripping from the adding machine a lengthy piece of tape, recalling how often I've seen my mother do the same, I hear her say: "So anyway, Michael, what did Mason have to say?"

"Not much. Sit down. I need to ask you a question Mom."

"What's that, Michael?"

"Did you give Michael any cash? Did you give Michael any money?"

"Michael I told him *Friday* night at the supper table that I was going to give him his birthday money. You were sitting there. You heard me say that."

"I missed it Mom."

"Well I said it. You can ask Beth if you don't believe me."

"I believe you. How much?"

"Fifty dollars."

"Did you give it to him yet?"

"Just before he went to bed last night."

Blinking back the blowing out of a blue votive light, I say: "You've got to take that money back Mom."

"Why?"

"Because Mason says Michael's begun to borrow money he can't pay back, that's why."

"But it's Michael's *birthday* money, Michael. I promised a long time ago to give it to him this weekend."

"I don't care Mom. You've got to take that money back. Michael's got to learn he's not going to have you around to help him out all the time."

"Well you're right about that Michael," she says. "I'm seventy-three years old. I'm not getting any younger."

Yes she is. Every time my mother says that she's seventy-three years old, that she's not getting any younger, her words, making her look about ten years younger, fill me with a sharp alcoholic hunger.

Swallowing it back, I say: "OK. Go on upstairs Mom. Send Michael down. He's going back to Iowa broke."

"Well Michael," she says, "you're Michael's father. You're the boss. You know what's best."

Then she's gone up the stairs and Michael is slamming down them, screaming: "Goddamn it Dad. What did you say to Grandma? She's crying. You made her cry."

"No I didn't Michael, you did."

"I did? How?"

Like this. Up the sidewalk of the house in Iowa comes again the ten-speed kid. This time he's on a very red, very high-seated Schwinn and even before he can triple-brake to a stop in front of Ray, I hear Michael say: "Ray? That faggot? That sneak? That creep? That's my *birthday* money you're talking about Dad."

"Not to repay a debt you shouldn't have incurred in the first place, it's not. That money's going back to your Grandma."

"Grandma doesn't *want* that money back Dad. And you can't make me give it back to her either."

Overhead the naked bulb is bright and standing toe-to-toe with Michael, I say, "Look Michael, I'm not afraid *of* you, I'm afraid *for* you."

"Jesus Dad," he says. "What does *that* mean?"

"That means, Michael, you just get your ass up those stairs and hand that money back to Grandma."

"*Make* me."

To make Michael give his birthday money back to his grandmother, to force his hand into his back pocket, to force my mother's hand to grasp a fifty-dollar bill she didn't want to grasp, to impose upon the two of them an object lesson, the object of which is slowly but completely losing itself upon me, is to draw from Michael a comment upon that loss.

Grunting, "Ah fuck," he slams up the basement stairs and, to the chuckle of the ghosts of taxpayers past, I follow him.

Hoping in a way to see Michael standing alone in the living room with a fifty-dollar bill clipped between his teeth, I imagine a second wrestle Michael and I might wrestle. Beginning with a hand-grapple and moving through armlock, hammerlock, then into full-nelson, it would conclude not so much with the spitting out by my son of my mother's money, as it would in the roseate nose, chin and ear abrasions of deep, deep carpet burn.

But when I get upstairs, I find that Michael's gone, that the house is empty.

Picking up my bag and walking out the door, I see that he and Beth are in the car, that my mother is standing at the open door on the driver's side, waiting for a good-bye kiss.

To kiss my mother good-bye is an orthopedic experience. Touching my lips to her forehead, I feel the thump of her feet on concrete, I walk once more the walk that took us this morning to and from church. Unable *not* to imperil that walk, unable, when I stationed myself outside church waiting for my mother until Mass was over, *not* to imagine ice on the sidewalks and purse snatchers behind the bushes, I look now into the car at Beth's bare feet.

Braced on the dashboard as if in anticipation of the dangers of the interstate, they fill me with the care I know I'm going to take in getting us safely back and forth today across the Mississippi River.

Ducking into the driver's seat, closing then locking the door, snapping my seat belt and starting the car, I know I'm about to get from my mother a word that will move this good-bye far beyond the Mississippi River.

That word is *Montana,* and get it I do. Leaning into the window, invoking the name of a state undoubtedly as tough as any in the country on Levi wear, she blinks her eyes and says: "Well Michael I hope you get a lot of good wear out of your Levis. Is Grandma going to get to see you again before you move to Montana?"

It is a question that, hitting a brake and throwing a seat release that I myself haven't touched, slams me into the steering wheel.

With his entire upper body wedged out the driver's side window, Michael wraps his grandmother in a hug so tight and heed-less of me, I fear the blast of a car horn against my chest.

Pushing away from a horn I feel within my heart, a horn about to blow, about to go, thinking: *Now you two stop that hugging, you're going to hurt me, you're going to hurt me,* I turn, having run out of turns, toward Beth.

The look she gives me, a look of scrutiny and fresh assess-ment, says unequivocally: Go.

To the pop of the clutch, to the thump of Michael's weight hit-ting the back seat, waving good-bye to good-bye-waving mother, we do, we go.

Room 601

Named after a saint and set upon a lake, this hospital, flying outside the black flag of its smokestack, keeps sneaking up on me, my family.

Particularly this room, Room 601. According to a plaque on the wall as you enter, the furnishings in this room were purchased with contributions made by the Purity Baking Company and its employees. The kind of fact that sticks in your mind, it is a fact that, given the present circumstances, sticks in my craw. Two aunts, an uncle and my father have died in this room and now the nuns have assigned it to my mother. There ought of course to be a law, some statute that would limit the number of Murphys assigned Room 601.

But there is no such statute and having been assigned it and having accepted quietly that assignment (along with, on my first visit to her, a whispered asking of me *please* not to mention it to the nun in charge), my mother has left all the gall up to me: *because I can't stand it* that the nuns have assigned my mother Room 601, I tell myself that it is absolutely crucial that, if I am to come to an understanding of what it means to be my mother's son, I have not only to accept, but even savor the fact that the nuns have assigned my mother Room 601.

Suspect, unsavory, the thought sends a tremor through my mother.

From it she awakens to roll her eyes, squeeze my hand and

whisper: "Whatever you do Michael, take care of your kidneys. Don't drink too much."

"I don't drink too much Mom."

"Then don't drink to excess, Michael."

Ah, the pressure of her hand, the beauty of her mind as she mothers me. Because it might drive me to drink, I try not to think about a distinction in my mother's mind between "too much" and "to excess." Instead, nodding my head, I say: "OK Mom, I promise. Now try to go back to sleep."

In the folding of her hands across her chest, in the closing of her eyes, there is something so quick, childlike and obedient, a need so strong to mind, to be good, to obey, her eyelids begin after only a moment to quiver. Then they pop open.

Tightening her grip once more on my hand, she says: "Michael, I want to ask you a question."

I say: "Sure, Mom" and she says: "Michael, are we wasting time?"

"What do you mean, Mom, are we wasting time?"

"I mean with you and this room and these flowers and the nuns and the nurses and the doctors, are we wasting time?"

"No Mom, we're not wasting time."

"Then what about this?"

"What about what?"

Sticking her hip with a fingertip, she thumbs down an imaginary plunger and says: "This."

"That's Demerol, Mom. It's to let you sleep. It's to let you relax."

"Are you sure Michael?"

I say: "Sure I'm sure," but I might just as well have said: *shush.*

My mother, having heard an admonition rather than an answer, falls so suddenly back to sleep, I know she's right to worry about my drinking. I am so afraid of Room 601, so afraid of the death my mother's dying in it, so ashamed and amazed by her sense of importuning me and the nuns and nurses and doctors with her dying, I am dying for a drink. I cannot wait for one.

Instead, I get a call on the intercom. Crackling, the intercom says: "Murphy, do you want communion?"

By "Murphy" the intercom means, of course, my mother not me. But because I have never in my life heard anyone call my mother "Murphy," because I myself have often answered to the male and cursory name of "Murphy," it is as if the intercom has asked me and not my mother if I want communion.

I do not. I want gin. Perhaps if I asked just right, a very dry, very cold gin martini would appear in my hand. Whispering a toast to Purity Baking Company and its employees, I'd tip it up and feel Room 601 expand. Up the walls and across the ceiling would run a memorial to all the Murphys who have died here. Sistine and star-studded, a study dominated by my dead father reaching down an index finger to pull my mother up into a heaven she could enter without a second thought to me and my apostate sister, all that blue and gold Michaelangelic space would ease a claustrophobia the intercom insists upon.

"Murphy," it repeats, "do you want communion?"

I am not a religious person. But I am a superstitious one. And though I no longer believe in the divinity of Jesus Christ, nor in the changing of a wafer of bread into his body and blood, I do believe in threes.

So does the intercom. Having asked me twice if I want communion, it asks me a third. "Murphy," it says, "do you want communion?"

It is, I have to admit, a good question. If I say "yes," two things will happen: my mother will get communion and I will get my just deserts—onto a list the nuns keep somewhere in the basement of St. Mary's Hospital, a list of potential deathbed Catholics, my name will be added. I do not want my name added. But the intercom does. Crackling, the intercom says: "Murphy in Room 601, do you want communion?"

"Yes."

"Yes?"

"*Yes.*"

My answer, recorded in the book of the dead of Room 601, brings down the house. Overhead, a whole mural of dead Murphys contracts with laughter and my mother awakens to a thirst more simple than mine: "Michael," she says, "I want a glass of tap water."

From the bathroom, I get it for her. When, propping up her head, I offer the glass to her, she neither drinks nor sips, but merely wets her lips. Then blinking and shaking her head, she says: "Was that tap water?"

"That was tap water."

"Well that's what I wanted," she says, "tap water. Now I'm going to get myself a little rest."

As if to add an amen to my mother's intention, the intercom says: "Could I have your attention please? Visiting hours are over at 8 P.M. It is now 8 P.M."

Sitting abruptly up, my mother says: "Michael, have you got your list?"

Taking a slip of paper from my pocket, I say: "Right here, Mom."

"Good. Because Hope's here so you better be going."

My mother can't be right, but she is. In a chair behind me and to my right, sits Hope with her tic. At first I misinterpreted it. When I entered my mother's room and saw Hope sitting there clicking her knitting needles and ever so slightly shaking her head, I shook my head back at her, as if to acknowledge some new symptom or marked erosion of my mother's condition. Then when she looked back at her knitting, I saw that the shaking of her head was metronomic, no more communicative than the tiny bit of gum she was so lightly, softly working.

She works it now. Kissing my mother on the forehead, squeezing her hand, I say: "I love you, Momma, I'll take care of the list."

Then backing up from the bed and shaking my head at head-shaking Hope, holding in my right fist a crumpled list concluding with a note to call my sister Martha, I all but stumble out of Room 601.

❖ ❖ ❖

In winter the soybean processing plants of Decatur come out in technicolor, flap the white, blue and chartreuse flags of their smokestacks. At night these stacks look spot-lit and walking toward my mother's house, I am tempted *not* to call my sister Martha.

Also I am tempted to litter. In my left fist, shoved deep in my jacket pocket, I carry another piece of paper. It is a fold of unused toilet tissue from the bathroom of Room 601 and fingering it I endure an old sense of sanctum sanctorum.

Certain there are certain places I should never in my life have grown old enough to go, I stand once more as I stood earlier this evening, beside my toilet-sitting mother. Hoping to feel through the thinness of her shoulder, a rattle of urination however faint, I look at the chain on the wall of the bathroom of Room 601. It says: "Pull For Help" and staring at it, I wonder as I've often wondered, what would happen if I pulled it.

Though I know only a nun or nurse would appear to ask what was the matter, I cannot help but imagine the arrival in Room 601 of St. Mary's Hospital of my sister Martha. If Mom needed any help with the carefully folded toilet tissue I hold in my hand, Martha would take care of that.

But I do not pull the "Pull For Help" chain and my mother cannot pee. Rising with my help, she turns toward the mirror and though she purses, then smacks her lips, she doesn't comment on the lopsidedness of her lipstick. Instead she simply looks.

There is a word for how my mother looks. That word is "awful." It is also the word, in our family, for cancer. On her one and only trip down from Minneapolis, Martha was the first member of the family to use it. As soon as she hugged and kissed her, as soon as she straightened Mom's lopsided lipstick and confirmed for herself that the nuns had assigned her Room 601, Martha drew me into the hallway and whispered: "My god Michael.

Mom looks *awful*. Are you *sure* the doctor hasn't said anything about cancer?"

A question I knew Martha would ask me, it is based on an article of faith, an Irish Catholic sense of the clinical.

In our family if you're a widow over the age of seventy and you smoke and drink and go to daily Mass, then the only thing that can kill you is cancer and the only word for that is "awful."

Mom, though, has managed to look "awful" and not have cancer. According to her doctor, she suffers from an "impaired renal artery" and "pulmonary edema." This evening her kidneys were functioning at "only 42 percent capacity" and she was, the doctor said, "close to, but not yet into uremia."

Thinking of uremia as a country small, dark and hard as the Emerald Isle itself, a place you'd need only to show a ticket of unused toilet tissue to enter, I drop the toilet tissue into a storm drain, turn and mount with a bound the front steps of my mother's house.

Unlocking the triple-locked door, I let myself in and head immediately for the kitchen.

On a shelf to the left of the sink, just next to a half-filled bottle of Oil of Olay, there sits a music box which, if I lifted its lid, would play "Galway Bay."

I know "Galway Bay" by heart. So does my mother. But she could not know this. In her absence from a house we both know by heart, in her removal to a hospital room we both know by heart, I have given in to mindlessness. Tempted to lift the lid of a green-jeweled music box, to annoint my hands with Oil of Olay while at the same time I intone the words of "Galway Bay," a song that would set heaven in Ireland, I turn toward the liquor cabinet.

Working with olives and toothpicks and a cut-glass shot glass, gratified by the dumb glug-glug of the near-full half-gallon bottle of gin with its built-in pour spout, I make myself a martini in the dark.

It is a very large one on the rocks and with it I intend to walk into the even darker living room to call my sister, Martha.

When, long distance, I describe to her Mom's sticking of her hip with a fingertip, the plunger will thumb down on gin, not Demerol. To Martha I'll report so gravely our mother's question about wasting time, we'll both forget for awhile who's paying for the call.

Mom, of course, will be paying for the call. Upon that catch and contradiction, a sense of spending our mother's money to share her sense, in dying, of wasting our time, the telephone very loudly rings.

I do not want to answer it but, martini in hand, I do. Striding across the living room, I snap it up and say "hello" just a little louder than I wanted to.

"Hello," the voice says. "Is that you Michael?"

"Yes."

"Can you hold on a second?"

I can, but they can't. On the other end of the line, I hear a muffled bam, then the scrambling of a hand and the voice says: "Michael, I dropped the phone. Whew. I'm glad I got you. Hope here. Listen."

It isn't easy for me to listen. Against Hope's words, I hear the words I hoped to be speaking at this very moment to Martha: because I could not wait to needle Martha with a fingertip to the hip, to frighten her with Mom's question about wasting time, my mother has wasted very little time. She's had, out in Room 601, a breathing attack, a severe one. Also, in the hip, she's taken a shot not of gin, but Demerol.

"The nurse just left," I hear Hope say. "They've got the oxygen hooked up and your mother's calming down."

"I'll be there right away."

"No rush. I'm here. I'm holding her hand."

Upon the martini in my hand, Hope's words have a profound effect. Also, vaguely, a religious one: if I do not do what I've said that I'll do, if I do not get back there right away, I'll throw away my right to be my mother's son, to be as frightened as I can be by the breathing attack, a severe one, she's suffered out in Room 601. I do not want to throw that right away. Nor do I want to throw away my martini.

Nonetheless, I say: "OK Hope, I'm on my way." Then I slam the phone down and head back to the kitchen.

By the mindless shrine to the left of the sink, by Oil of Olay and "Galway Bay," I do not believe that I can transubstantiate a martini.

I do believe, though, that I can adulterate one. Recalling all the gall I've felt at my mother's assignment to Room 601, willing it to liquify, to return to its original bilious state, I try to pull it up from my liver, down my right arm, through my fingertips, into my martini.

It works, it gets me through, I do it. I sniff my glass, I wrinkle my nose, I shake my head, I thrust it from me. I pour my martini untouched down the kitchen drain.

It is not a moral gesture, it's only an effective one. By it, I feel sickened, shaken, frightened. Drawing from the faucet a tall glass of very cold tap water, thinking: *This is no joke, this is no laugher, I've got to shag my ass back out there,* I down it with a single gulp, turn and head as fast as I can for Room 601.

If prescience is impatient with the present, if it would make of nuns, nurses, doctors and even Demerol, nothing but a waste of time, then I can't take my eyes off the little blue oxygen bottle that gurgles and percs on the wall above my mother's bed.

Thinking, almost praying: *a watched pot never boils, a watched pot never boils,* I feel my mother's hand flinch in mine.

Fluttering open her eyes, she says: "After you left, Michael, I couldn't get my breath."

"I know, Mom. Hope called. She got me at home."

"She did?"

"Yes and I got here as fast as I could."

"Good, Michael, because I want to ask you a question."

"What's that Mom?"

"Will you pray with me?"

"Will I pray with you?"

"Yes, Michael, will you pray with me?"

Saying: "Sure, Mom," I lower my eyes and enact with my mother a little lie. I don't think my mother really expects me to pray with her. I think she only expects me to pretend to pray with her. To do so is both embarrassing and intimate. Also it is stirring. In the sharp metacarpals of her hand, I feel not only the bones of all the rosaries I know she's prayed for me, I feel the twist of my wrist above the kitchen sink.

Tempted to lean down and whisper: *I offered a martini to you, Mom, I poured it untouched down the drain,* I am thinking of an offering that would see, upon her death, my mother's soul directly to heaven, when I hear her say: "I don't want to go to heaven."

"What did you say, Mom?"

"I said I don't want to go to heaven, Michael. If you and Martha aren't going to be there with me, then I don't want to go to heaven either."

Because I cannot stand to hear my mother say she doesn't want to go to heaven if Martha and I aren't going to be there with her, the way that statement seems to paint her so permanently and tightly into her place on the ceiling above my head, I wish Martha were here to hear what our mother just said. I am thinking: *Martha would think of something to say* when, waking from a sleep into which I hadn't realized she'd slipped, my mother says: "Michael, when you were home just now, did you call Martha?"

"I was going to, Mom, but Hope got me first and I thought I'd better get back here right away."

Whispering: "Oh, OK," she falls back to sleep and I hear Hope say what she's said to me a couple of times already: if I want to slip out into the hall to call Martha, she'll take over, she'll watch my mother, she'll hold her hand.

Though I haven't seen her take it, Hope is already holding my mother's other hand and frightened by my need to frighten my sister, to hustle down the hall to call Martha in Minneapolis, to shout out a recrimination about a heaven to which Mom doesn't want to go if the two of us aren't going to be there with her, I'm afraid that if I try to step out the door, Hope will stop me again, will call me for a final time back to Room 601.

She does. I'm halfway to the pay phone down the hall, digging in my pocket for change, when I hear behind me the conjugation of a verb.

From the doorway of Room 601, Hope calls out: "Michael, I don't think you'd better go. I think your mother's going. I think your mother might be gone."

Hope's wrong. When I reenter Room 601, my mother sits bolt upright and says: "Oh, Gerald, is that you?"

Gerald is my mother's dearly loved younger brother, a plain-clothes cop dead at age forty-five of a heart attack and when my mother calls me by his name, I feel him slip from his place on the ceiling of Room 601.

Breaking out of the handcuffs that handcuff him to the heart attack that killed him, leaving behind his lieutenancy in the po-lice force, the cortège of light-blinking squad cars that trailed his hearse to the cemetery, leaving behind six children and a wife, he slides down the wall of Room 601 to take my mother's hand.

I am holding my mother's hand and telling myself that it's against the law to impersonate a police officer, to interfere in the performance of his last official act, I hear my mother ask me again if I'm my uncle.

I am not a religious person, but I am a suggestible one. And though I no longer believe in the priestliness of police work, no longer see my uncle as a saint in a snap-brim hat dead of a heart attack that cuffed his hands behind his back, I do believe in threes.

So does my mother. Having asked me twice if I'm my uncle, she asks me a third. "Oh, Gerald," she says, "is that you?"

It is, I have to admit, a good question. If I say "yes," two things will happen: I will get my badge, handcuffs and snub-nosed .38 and my uncle will get himself a drink. Seeing him as a priest from green uremia adulterating a martini over the kitchen sink, I feel the color drain from my face.

It's my uncle's face that's done most of the draining and when I begin to feel a little faint, I hear him say: *That's better. Way better. Just keep that same expression on your face. We can begin now with the glowing of the green.*

It begins around my mother's mouth and extends outward. Faintly, lowly, my mother begins to glow green, and when she can glow no lower, when the gap of her mouth can get no blacker, she loosens her grip on my hand, she rises with her called down younger brother to assume the place prepared for her on the ceiling of Room 601.

Finding My Niche

I AM ten years old and having trouble with math. So much trouble in fact that I am serving this afternoon a kind of detention, sitting at the kitchen table trying to make sense of long division.

I can't. Into my remainders, my divisors won't go and after awhile I experience true excruciation: through me shoots a little panic that, stopping in the penis, snaps the pencil in my hand. I have never before snapped a pencil in my hand and thrilled and appalled by the glassy shatter of lead and wood, the miniature baseball bat complete with oval black trademark that I've broken, a word crackles through my mind. That word is *cocksucker* and though I don't know its precise meaning and have never spoken it before, its *c*'s and *k*'s seem so completely to correspond to my problem with long division, I know I am about to try the word on my income tax–frazzled mother.

I do.

Up the basement stairs she comes. In the beat of her feet there is the chatter of the typewriter, the thud of the adding machine.

When she arrives at the kitchen table and asks me what's the matter, I point my broken pencil at the paper in front of me and say: "I can't get this cocksucker, Mom."

"What?"

"I tried, Mom," I say, "but I just can't get this cocksucker."

My mother does not slap me intentionally on the ear, but that's where, palm cupped, some thirty years ago, her hand whams my head.

Good, good. It is a blow that stands me up. To the slap of my hand against the kitchen table, murmuring the *c*'s and *k*'s of the word I've tried and failed to get past my income tax–frazzled mother, I get from her a question I somehow knew she'd ask. "Where, young man," she says, "did you get such language?"

Where indeed. Searching the kitchen wall for the face of the man from whom I first heard the word *cocksucker* spoken in anger, I arrive after a moment at a drunken uncle. His name is Charlie and as he hurls an unfixable clock against the wall of his fix-it shop, I hear him scream the word *cocksucker* so hard it brings, at about its fifth or sixth enunciation, my Uncle Charlie to his knees.

But I do not tell my mother this. Instead I scream what I cannot help but scream: "Why did you have to hit me?"

"I hit you, young man, because you will not use that kind of language in this house."

"What kind of language?"

"You know perfectly well what kind of language."

Yes, I guess I do. Impetuously, experimentally, I have tried to use in front of my mother a word I hoped might work like a vacuum cleaner. *Cocksucker,* though, doesn't pull from the paper in front of me, the doodles and delirium of a problem in long division. It draws from my mother, some thirty years ago, another word that gives me trouble.

That word is *apply.* Just before she turns back to the basement and the income tax business she conducts down there, she says: "Now you get, young man, right back to work, you *apply* yourself do you hear me, you *apply* yourself."

I can't apply myself. Neither, I think, can Uncle Charlie. Sometimes when I sit with him in his fix-it shop, I hear him mutter from the manuals with which he's attempting to repair the irreparable mangle irons, toasters and sewing machines he's promised his customers he'll fix. These manuals are filled with the word *apply* and sometimes Uncle Charlie mutters the word so often and so breathlessly I know his hands are about to begin to tremble, that, mangling a customer's mangle iron, he'll mangle himself, Uncle Charlie will apply the skin and blood of his knuckles to his workbench.

I feel the same way about math.

I know that I cannot work my problem in long division with my fists. But when my mother tells me to *apply* myself do I hear her, *apply* myself, the word makes me want to apply my fists to the kitchen table.

Feeling in my hand the pencil-snapping panic that, with only a little help from Uncle Charlie, sent the word *cocksucker* crackling across my mind, I feel I've been done, by the wham of my mother's hand against my ear, a deep injustice. Wanting to call her back upstairs and to say: *I didn't come up with the word* cocksucker, *Mom, my penis did,* I think that if I were to truly apply myself to math, that application might somehow involve my penis.

After awhile it does.

I am by now thirteen and a half years old and unable to come up with another word for my problem in math, I'm stuck with one that, continuing to snap pencils in my hand, frees my penis from my pants.

I now know full well what the word *cocksucker* means and when, slamming me to my knees, my application to math seems most total, I feel like I'm about to break my back trying to perform on myself an unnatural act for which my mother, storming up from the basement, provides a final word.

That word is *handicapped,* but I am so busy scrambling back up into my chair, so busy zipping my pants, I hear near nothing until I hear my mother say: "Did you hear, young man, a word I said?"

"You said you give up on me in math. You said I'm hopeless. You said I'm handicapped."

"That's right, *handicapped*. You've permanently *handicapped* yourself in math and a person never outgrows that kind of handicap. If you don't believe me just come down and ask half the taxpayers in this basement."

I don't want to. If I followed my mother down the stairs, I might see in the faces of half the taxpayers in the basement, the face of Uncle Charlie. Mangled by the mangle irons he's mangled, undermined in the mouth and clouded in the eyes by the *c*'s and *k*'s of a word he can't stop screaming, Uncle Charlie's face, like the faces of half the taxpayers in the basement, bears the look of a man deeply handicapped in math.

I don't want to grow up like Uncle Charlie. Nor do I want to grow up like my mother either. Sometimes when the pencil snaps, when the panic truly crackles, I think that if I ever *did* grasp math, it might earn me a place in the basement alongside my mother making out income tax.

Though she never quite says so, I think she would like to see me someday take just such a place. Often on Saturday nights, after the basement empties itself at last of taxpayers, she lights a cigarette and pops open with a church key, an ice-cold can of beer. Then she does something I wish she wouldn't do. She has herself a little laugh at the taxpayers' expense. Especially at Uncle Charlie's.

"That Charlie," she sighs and says. "He can't add, subtract, multiply or divide, but he sure can sign his name. That man couldn't wait to sign his name and get out of here. If you don't believe me, just go down and look into the front window of The Niche."

The Niche is our neighborhood tavern, not a block from our house and when she points me toward it, my mother points directly at a holy picture on the wall.

It depicts the Pentecost and through it, without ever walking down there, I can see very clearly into the front window of The Niche at Uncle Charlie.

Over his head, in the shape of a tongue of flame, hangs the

shame of having signed again this year, an income tax return he does not understand. This shame makes him thirsty and edgy and when the tongue above his head begins to call for a licking, he cocks his fist and, intent above all on missing my mother, determined above all to keep my mother out of this, he swings and hits the man standing next to him.

The man standing next to him is another taxpayer from my mother's basement and when Uncle Charlie's fist intersects with his face, a kind of tying of tongues takes place.

Above their heads a double tongue of flame whips round and round the *c*'s and *k*'s of a single phrase. That phrase is *cocksucking suckerpunch*. And when under its Pentecostal spit, Uncle Charlie seems engaged less in a fight than in a deep fit of math handicap, I know that, staring through the front window of The Niche, I'm staring at my own future as a barroom brawler, a thrower of fists over which, as a blind signer of my own blind name, I have as little control as Uncle Charlie.

I am forty years old and having trouble again with math. So much trouble in fact that I can't meet the eyes of the man to whom I've come this afternoon for outside help. He is an attorney, a specialist in inheritance law, and adding power to the power of attorney he's already granted me, he issues me, the attorney does, a checkbook.

This is the second such checkbook he's given me, and taking it from him, I take another lesson in math. "Do you know," he says, "how to close out a checking account?"

"I'm not sure."

"OK," he says, "I'll show you."

Show me he does. Through canceled and outstanding checks, through bank statements and slips of deposit and withdrawal, through all of the fanned and annotated papers spread out before us, the attorney whips so quickly I want, when he strikes his balance on the very first try, to reach out and take a swing at him.

But I do no such thing. Instead, I do what the attorney asks me to do. I write out a check to him for the entire amount remaining in an account for which I've been named executor, an account entitled The Estate of Helen Martha Murphy.

As I do so, the attorney makes a point of law I've heard him make a couple of times before.

At the moment of death, he tells me, a person's assets automatically and instantaneously freeze. He seems fond of this law and knowing that he's talking about my mother's death, my mother's assets, knowing that she too would have liked such a law, one that, blending thrift with refrigeration, stopped, when she died, a lot of numbers absolutely cold, I feel like I'm holding in my hand not a ballpoint pen, but an axe or ball-peen hammer. Tools that might draw from my mouth the *c*'s and *k*'s of a word I wouldn't want to speak in front of an attorney, a word that might bloody and botch the iced-up lock the law has placed on my mother's assets, I am trying to look up and meet his eye, when I hear the attorney say: *easy*.

"What did you say?"

"I said I know this isn't easy. The settling of an estate can be a complicated business. Particularly when it involves the sale of a business like your mother's income tax business. Now you're sure you understand the figures on that?"

"I understand them all right."

"And the figures on your share of the estate?"

"Yes."

"No questions?"

"No."

"Because I want you to take your time. I don't want you to feel rushed. I don't want you to sign anything you don't understand."

Neither does my mother. Still tense for the tenths of percent by which, miraculously understanding fractions, I might throw off my handicap in math, she understands how, blindly signing in an attorney's office a check for a legal fee *I do not understand,* I might blindly sign to fight in a fight which, even as I hurry toward it, I incompletely understand.

The attorney, however, has no understanding of such matters. Smiling and accepting my check for his fee, a check that completely closes out an account he's explained to me that we *have to* completely close out, he doesn't notice the raising above my head of my mother's right hand.

I notice it, though, and when it whams my head, it tags with an earring the ear of a man standing at a bar some six blocks away from the attorney's office.

This earring is made of rhinestone and even as I smile and pump the attorney's hand, even as I thank him once or twice too often, I seem to swing open the door of a bar in the middle of which is standing, exactly where he ought to be, not a man with a rhinestone earring in his ear, but a man wearing a sleeveless white T-shirt.

When I find myself thinking: *he don't care what Momma don't allow, he's gonna wear his T-shirt anyhow,* I know that I should turn and leave. But I do not. Instead, I walk up to the bar and ask for trouble. I ask, that is, for a very dry martini on the rocks with a lemon twist.

Sometimes the mere smell of a martini, the quiet of the ice, the clarity of the gin, the pallor of the lemon rind will remind me that for reasons racial, even prenatal, I am someone who should never sniff, let alone sip a martini. But sip it I do.

As if on cue, I hear the *c*'s and *k*'s of the word I guess I came here to hear. I try to let it slip, but when a leather-coated man slips an arm over the shoulder of the T-shirted man, I cannot help but notice.

Noticing the drape of the leather arm over the T-shirted shoulder, the way both clash with the clothes and comportment of the attorneys, insurance agents and real estate men who inhabit this house of gin and tweed and law and real estate, I know that, before I hear my word again, I should turn and leave.

But again I do not. Instead, double-timing my martini and calling for another, I hear the T-shirted man say: "Don't do that."

"Don't do what?"

"Don't try to put words in my mouth."

"I'm not trying to put words in your mouth."

Yes he is. I think the leather-coated man is trying to put into the mouth of the T-shirted man the word I tried and failed, some thirty years ago, to get past my income tax–frazzled mother. When I think about that, I feel again the wham of a hand against my ear and something funny happens to my face.

My face begins to rattle. In my nose and brow, unbroken bones begin to snap, pop, call for cracking. Around my cheekbones and the sockets of my eyes, bull's-eyes begin to whisper: *rectify, rectify.*

It is a word that makes my mother nibble her knuckles. Knocking back my second martini and calling for a third, I watch the leather-coated man, using my word again, give the T-shirted man a little squeeze.

Nobody likes trouble. Especially my mother. Not even she, though, can deny the undeniable: in the right mouth, accompanied by a squeeze, my word can sound ugly indeed.

The leather-coated man has got the right mouth. In his mouth my word sounds so ugly I wish in a way the T-shirted man would just get up and leave. But he doesn't just get up and leave and when he shakes his head and asks the leather-coated man please to get his arm off his shoulder, the leather-coated man, using my word again, gives him another squeeze.

Nobody likes a bully. Not even my mother. But when, knocking back my third martini and calling for a fourth, I turn toward the leather-coated man, she gives a little shudder that says: *I think you'd do anything to hide your handicap in math. Don't reach out and tap that man on the shoulder.*

Reaching out and tapping the leather-coated man on the shoulder, I open my mouth and hear my mother say: *you have a terrible, terrible handicap in math.*

"What did you say?"

"I said why don't you just cut the crap? Why don't you just take your arm off his shoulder?"

"Are you going to make me?"

"Yep."

It is, I guess, a gaseous kind of answer. Above my head burps on a bluish tongue of flame and even before it can spit out the *c*'s and *k*'s of my deep mathematical shame, I hit as hard as I can the leather-coated man square in the face.

I have never before hit a man square in the face and thrilled and appalled that my fist has caught him in the mouth, I'm not surprised that, putting words into her mouth, gin and rage would have my mother whisper: *hit him again, Michael, kill the cocksucker.*

Such language is, of course, below my mother. So am I. Tempted to look up to see if she's still with me, I see that, astraddle the leather-coated man, I've got both his wrists pinned very tightly to the floor. It feels *good* to pin his wrists so tightly to the floor, but I am thinking: *what next Mom,* when I hear the leather-coated man say: "You suckerpunching cocksucker let me up. Why did you hit me?"

I hit you because you will not use, young man, that kind of language in this house.

"What? Who *are* you anyway?"

I am thinking: *I am the monster my mother never meant to make of me with math,* when I hear the leather-coated man scream: "You crazy fuck. I said let me up. What kind of number are you trying to *pull*?"

Trying to pull from the very air a number for the number that I'm trying to pull, I come up with the number for the cops.

I don't know the number for the cops. But the bartender does. So, in a way, does the T-shirted man.

Dropping a hand onto my shoulder, he says: "You'd better let him up. The bartender called the cops. They'll be here any minute."

A minute, I know, contains sixty seconds, sixty quick ticks of the clock. And though I'm still no good at all with numbers, I *can* add, I *can* subtract. Adding the fifteen or twenty ticks that have already passed, subtracting that from sixty, I'm figuring I've got maybe forty seconds between now and the arrival of the cops, when my mother stops me.

Cupping a hand to my right ear, she whispers: *That's enough math. Get up. Get out of here. For lo, Michael, he who would abet you is already at hand.*

Even as my mother speaks, the door of the bar swings open and standing in it, holding it open, is my attorney.

It seems strange to think of him as my attorney, but stranger still to see the look on his face.

On his face there is a look that says, having fought in a fight out of which I could not possibly have kept my mother, having fulfilled the contract I so recently, so blindly signed, I'm free now to get up and leave.

I do. Looking from my attorney's face to the face of the man below me, I apply my fists so hard to the wrists of the leather-coated man he doesn't, when I rise above him, move an inch. Neither does anybody else.

Thinking: *I've found my niche and I've got to get out of here,* I do what my mother would have me do, I back toward the door, I nod at my attorney, I get out of here.

ILLINOIS SHORT FICTION

Crossings by Stephen Minot
A Season for Unnatural Causes by Philip F. O'Connor
Curving Road by John Stewart
Such Waltzing Was Not Easy by Gordon Weaver

Rolling All the Time by James Ballard
Love in the Winter by Daniel Curley
To Byzantium by Andrew Fetler
Small Moments by Nancy Huddleston Packer

One More River by Lester Goldberg
The Tennis Player by Kent Nelson
A Horse of Another Color by Carolyn Osborn
The Pleasures of Manhood by Robley Wilson, Jr.

The New World by Russell Banks
The Actes and Monuments by John William Corrington
Virginia Reels by William Hoffman
Up Where I Used to Live by Max Schott

The Return of Service by Jonathan Baumbach
On the Edge of the Desert by Gladys Swan
Surviving Adverse Seasons by Barry Targan
The Gasoline Wars by Jean Thompson

Desirable Aliens by John Bovey
Naming Things by H. E. Francis
Transports and Disgraces by Robert Henson
The Calling by Mary Gray Hughes

Into the Wind by Robert Henderson
Breaking and Entering by Peter Makuck
The Four Corners of the House by Abraham Rothberg
Ladies Who Knit for a Living by Anthony E. Stockanes

Pastorale by Susan Engberg
Home Fires by David Long
The Canyons of Grace by Levi Peterson
Barbaru by B. Wongar

Bodies of the Rich by John J. Clayton
Music Lesson by Martha Lacy Hall
Fetching the Dead by Scott R. Sanders
Some of the Things I Did Not Do by Janet Beeler Shaw

Honeymoon by Merrill Joan Gerber
Tentacles of Unreason by Joan Givner
The Christmas Wife by Helen Norris
Getting to Know the Weather by Pamela Painter

Birds Landing by Ernest Finney
Serious Trouble by Paul Friedman
Tigers in the Wood by Rebecca Kavaler
The Greek Generals Talk by Phillip Parotti

Singing on the Titanic by Perry Glasser
Legacies by Nancy Potter
Beyond This Bitter Air by Sarah Rossiter
Scenes from the Homefront by Sara Vogan

Tumbling by Kermit Moyer
Water into Wine by Helen Norris
The Trojan Generals Talk by Phillip Parotti
Playing with Shadows by Gloria Whelan

Man without Memory by Richard Burgin
The People Down South by Cary C. Holladay
Bodies at Sea by Erin McGraw
Falling Free by Barry Targan

Private Fame by Richard Burgin
Middle Murphy by Mark Costello
Lives of the Fathers by Steven Schwartz